21x9/11 LT 10/09

Also by Luiz Alfredo Garcia-Roza

The Silence of the Rain
December Heat
Southwesterly Wind
A Window in Copacabana

Pursuit

Pursuit

Luiz Alfredo
GARCIA-ROZA

translated by Benjamin Moser

Henry Holt and Company
New York

Henry Holt and Company, LLC
Publishers since 1866
175 Fifth Avenue
New York, New York 10010

Henry Holt® and 🎪® are registered trademarks of
Henry Holt and Company, LLC.

Originally published in Brazil in 2003 under the title *Perseguido*
by Companhia das Letras, São Paulo

Library of Congress Cataloging-in-Publication Data
García-Roza, L. A. (Luiz Alfredo)
  [Perseguido. English]
  Pursuit : an Inspector Espinosa mystery / Luiz Alfredo García-Roza ;
translated by Benjamin Moser.
    p.   cm.
  ISBN-13: 978-0-8050-7439-0
  ISBN-10: 0-8050-7439-2
  I. Moser, Benjamin. II. Title
PQ9698.17.A745P4713 2006
869.3'42—dc22   2005046090

Henry Holt books are available for special promotions and
premiums. For details contact: Director, Special Markets.

First U.S. Edition 2006

Printed in the United States of America
1   3   5   7   9   10   8   6   4   2

Pursuit

On that hot December afternoon, his long strides and fixed stare didn't make it any easier to weave through all the pedestrians. To avoid bumping into people, and to maintain his steady rhythm, Espinosa found himself walking long stretches with one foot on the curb and the other in the street. He wasn't late for anything and he wasn't heading anywhere in particular. On the Rua da Quitanda, he had planned to turn onto the Rua do Carmo in order to check out the used-book store he'd visited since his law school days. But at the quick pace he was going, the Rua do Carmo and the bookstore were forgotten. Whenever possible, Espinosa took advantage of quiet afternoons at the station to examine a new bookstore or revisit one of his old haunts in the colonial buildings downtown. That was when he was working, but this afternoon he was just trying to enjoy one of his last days of vacation. The previous days hadn't differed much from the one that was already halfway over.

Things had started going south a week before the beginning of his vacation, when Irene had received an invitation to a two-week seminar at the Museum of Modern Art in New York. It came, out of the blue, from the museum itself, extended to foreign professionals who had distinguished themselves in some way over the last few years. So their own holiday, a trip to a beach in the Northeast, had had no choice but to relocate to Rio, which, after all, had beaches too. Great for Irene, a disaster for him. Great, too, for highlighting the difference between a graphic designer and a police chief, he thought, picking up the pace even more.

He'd been wandering through the downtown streets for almost two hours. In one of his hands he carried a small bag with two books he'd bought that afternoon, but he no longer remembered their titles, or even where he'd bought them. He didn't have much interest either in the snack he'd planned to enjoy at the Confeitaria Colombo. It was Thursday and he didn't have to be back at work until Monday. He headed to the nearest subway station and returned home.

The phone rang for the first time at seven-twenty that evening. Over the next fifteen minutes, it rang twice more. But nobody spoke on the other end of the line. Espinosa hesitated before picking up the fourth time, and when he did he met the same silence he'd encountered the first three times. He was about to hang up when he heard a man's voice.

"Chief Espinosa?"

"Yes."

"I'm sorry to be calling you at home, but at the station they said you were on vacation."

"That's true."

"My name is Artur Nesse. I'm a doctor. . . . A colleague at the hospital gave me your name. . . . You helped him . . ."

". . . and now you need my help."

"Right. . . . Well, not me, exactly . . . somebody else. . . . But I really don't know what to do. Excuse me, Officer, I'm feeling really confused."

"I'm going back to work on Monday. Why don't you come by then to tell me what's going on?"

"I can't wait until then. . . . It's urgent. . . . It's my daughter . . ."

"What happened to your daughter?"

"She disappeared . . . kidnapped."

"She disappeared or she was kidnapped?"

"First she disappeared, then I saw she'd been kidnapped."

"And how did you see she'd been kidnapped?"

"Well . . . it's obvious."

"How long ago did she disappear?"

"One day. A day and a night."

"How old is your daughter?"

"Seventeen."

"Have you had any contact with her since she disappeared?"

"No, none."

"So how do you know that she was kidnapped?"

"Because there's no other explanation."

"Have you already informed the kidnapping police?"

"No! I don't want my daughter mixed up with the police."

"Do you want her involved with kidnappers?"

"Can we speak personally?"

"We already are speaking personally."

"I mean face-to-face. They told me you're a considerate man."

"I am, but my consideration makes me reluctant to believe that your daughter's been kidnapped."

"Why do you think that?"

"Because if you thought your daughter had been kidnapped, you wouldn't be doing this. Maybe your daughter ran away from home."

"I'd like you to take on the case."

"Dr. Nesse, I'm a police officer, not a private investigator. If you want a private investigation, you should get in touch with a detective agency."

"Could we at least talk about the case? It's not just my daughter's disappearance. There are other things as well."

"Fine. I'll expect you in half an hour in the square in the Peixoto District, in Copacabana. Take down the address."

﹍

At that hour, the square was empty: the people who hung out there in the afternoon had left and the square had not received the contingent of people who arrived after dinner and the evening news. After waiting for fifteen minutes in the doorway of his building, Espinosa noticed a car making the whole loop around the square. It was a fancy imported sedan, seemingly new, its dark color shining beneath the reflections of the streetlights. The driver didn't look at the buildings, as if searching for a specific address, nor did he seem to be seeking out a specific person. On the second trip around the square he found a good parking place. Only then did he park, lock the door, circle the car once, and move off, looking at the buildings and a piece of paper he had in his hand.

Espinosa waited until the man was close to him before speaking.

"Dr. Nesse? I'm Chief Espinosa."

"Oh, sir, I was just looking for your building."

They shook hands. Dr. Nesse was only a little taller than Espinosa, but he seemed twice as large.

They walked across the street slowly and silently, looking for an isolated bench.

"So, Doctor, what happened?"

STORY NUMBER ONE

When the doctor came in, chart in hand, he encountered the kid already inside the examination room, staring through the blinds at the hospital's inner courtyard. That wasn't the way things were done. The assistant was only supposed to send the patient through once the doctor was already in the consultation room. The kid turned his head when he noticed the doctor coming in, glanced at him for a second, and then moved silently toward the middle of the room. They were about the same height: the kid was thin, a little bent over, with black hair and stubble. The doctor was fat, very pale, and a little too bald for his age.

"Hi there, I'm Dr. Nesse. You're Isidoro?"

"They call me Isidoro."

"Isidoro Cruz," the doctor said, checking his file.

"That's what they call me, but my name is Jonas."

The doctor pointed to one of the two chairs and took a seat in the other one, facing the only window of the small room.

"Why do they call you Isidoro if your name is Jonas?"

"Because that's what my parents wanted them to call me."

"But you prefer Jonas?"

"That's my name."

"So then your full name is Jonas Cruz?"

"No. My name is Jonas."

"And you don't have a last name?"

"Jonas is fine."

"And what's your parents' last name?"

"Cruz."

"Your real name, then, is Isidoro Cruz, but you'd rather be called Jonas. Just Jonas. How long ago did you decide that your name wasn't Isidoro Cruz?"

"Since I was small."

"And that's when you decided to change it?"

"No. I just decided not to be Isidoro anymore."

"And when did you start calling yourself Jonas?"

"When I was seventeen."

"Here on your chart it says you're twenty-two."

"That's right."

"What happened when you were seventeen to make you take the name Jonas?"

"Nothing when I was seventeen, but when I was thirteen."

"And what happened when you were thirteen?"

"Have we already started?"

"Started what?"

"The treatment."

"Well, this is just a preliminary interview. . . . You still haven't told me what's wrong."

"I came to resolve a personal matter."

"And does that matter involve the fact that you don't like your name?"

"That's just a detail."

"What's the main issue, then? Was it what happened when you were thirteen?"

"Maybe, but it's still difficult to talk about that."

"It might be easier to talk about next time," the doctor said, getting up from his chair and looking at the kid.

"Is that it?"

"Like I said, this is just a quick preliminary interview. We'll have others before we start the treatment. Today is Wednesday. I'll see you next Wednesday, at the same time."

Fifteen minutes had passed, if that. The kid had expected a little more out of the session. He said farewell to the doctor and left the room wondering what the next session would be like. He said good-bye to the receptionist as he walked through the entry hall, then crossed the patio toward the shaded street that led to the edge of the hospital grounds and the university campus. Once off campus, he kept walking, without looking at the bus stop or even glancing up to see if a bus was coming. He kept walking, indifferent to everything.

He was still thinking about the doctor's statement, that their encounter had only been preliminary. He wanted to think about the appointment and preferred to do so walking. He kept walking, crossing the tunnel connecting the neighborhoods of Botafogo and Copacabana, taking

a right on the Rua Barata Ribeiro, which crosses the
whole neighborhood, and followed that street to its end.
By the time he finished the walk, he still couldn't decide
if the doctor seemed suspicious.

At the second interview, Dr. Nesse had changed: his
eyes were more attentive and his speech less decisive.
Jonas immediately noticed the transformation.

"Hello, Isidoro. Have a seat."

"My name is Jonas, Doctor."

"When the receptionist scheduled your appointment
and opened your file, the name she got from your ID
card was Isidoro Cruz. Now you're saying that docu-
ment is wrong and that your name is Jonas. Just Jonas.
Apparently the main reason we're here is to resolve
this contradiction. From what I understand, you are
truly worried about this: you yourself came looking for
treatment, passed the hospital's screening procedures,
waited a long time to be helped, and are here of your
own volition."

"It's discomfiting to be called by a name that isn't
my own."

"Your parents must also be discomfited by your calling yourself a name they didn't give you."

"That's their problem, not mine. If I decide to call my
dog Fido, that doesn't mean that his name necessarily
has to be Fido, or that he's particularly faithful."

"Do you think you're hiding from something?"

"No, I'm trying to face it, which is why I sought treatment."

"The treatment hasn't yet begun. We're still in the introductory process. Your physical presence here is not enough to be called a treatment. You still haven't explained why you came."

"Doctor, if you say that I'm the one who has to ask to be helped, who would you be trying to help: Jonas or Isidoro?"

"That's a good start."

"If you decide what you're going to call me: Jonas or Isidoro."

The doctor's attitude, the way he conducted the conversation, and even his tone of voice were all different this time, but the most significant change was that the session lasted almost an hour. The only thing that was the same was the way it ended.

"That's enough for today. I'll see you next Wednesday."

As soon as the patient left, Dr. Nesse checked the address on his file. It was in Ipanema, not far from where he himself lived. Maybe that was why he had the feeling that he'd seen the guy somewhere. Maybe he'd noticed him on the street, or at the newspaper kiosk, even though he rarely walked through the neighborhood and didn't make a habit of hanging out at newspaper kiosks.

It made Jonas's job easier that the hospital was located on the university campus. The grounds surrounding the hospital itself were protected, and had only one entrance, but people moved around the area with relative ease. Some inpatients wandered around the campus, mingling with the students, without causing any disruption; some would even go into classrooms and sit with the students for a few minutes. He knew all this before he'd registered for the free consultation service the hospital offered, even before he started hanging out in the hospital garden every day in order to observe Dr. Nesse's movements.

It wasn't a meticulously kept garden, and a lot of it wasn't even kept at all, but it was fairly big, and some of its trees were a century old. Many of the patients approached him to ask for cigarettes or money. They didn't want much, just some change to get a soft drink in the cafeteria or to buy a box of cookies. They weren't poor, at least not most of them; but they were people who had been forgotten or abandoned by their families. This was the only annoyance they caused the students and teachers.

All he needed was a week, before starting his treatment, to learn everything he needed to know about Dr. Nesse's routine: his car, where he usually parked, which parts of the hospital he spent the most time in, as well as the fact that he had lunch in the hospital restaurant every day before leaving. Jonas learned all of this, but the doctor never noticed him.

The day of the third session was plagued with torrential rains. For vehicles heading downtown from Copacabana, traffic had nearly ground to a complete halt. Halfway through the neighborhood, the kid got off the bus and started walking. Some of the streets were completely flooded, and since it was high tide none of the water could drain off into the sea. On the sidewalk, people huddled underneath the awnings. Jonas arrived late at the hospital, soaking wet. Dr. Nesse still wasn't there, and judging by the small number of cars in the parking lot, many of the doctors and employees were stuck in traffic. By noon, the rain was less intense, but the doctor still hadn't arrived. He waited a little longer and decided to go back home.

On the bus, he thought about the next appointment and reflected that he would have to wait another week to learn the answers to the questions he had prepared. He wasn't worried about the delay; he wasn't in a hurry. As Dr. Nesse had said, they were only in the preliminary stages. And what difference did time make, when you already knew the ending?

The next morning, shielded by the blinds in the examination room, the doctor eyed the guy seated on the stone bench, beneath the mango tree, in the hospital courtyard. He didn't look aggressive, the doctor thought, at least not physically. Verbally, he'd already shown that he could speak well and hold his ground in discussions. In the last two weeks, he'd started showing up at the hospital every day, most of the time sitting underneath the big mango tree near the reception area. Every once in a while, he'd pace the courtyard or wander through some other part of the hospital, especially those areas designated for patients' recreation. He wasn't going out of his way to let himself be seen, but he wasn't hiding either. He had transformed the stone bench into a kind of control post, the doctor thought, only leaving it at the invitation of another patient. It wasn't the first time Dr. Nesse had found himself the target of a patient's curiosity, and he knew that in most cases the patient's interest represented only a passing phase. Since the examination room was small, the doctor preferred to keep the blinds open, so that he could see outside and make the room feel a little bigger. But ever since the guy had started using the bench outside as an observation post, he'd kept the blinds closed.

"If you'd like, we could send him to another doctor."

"No. In fact, he still hasn't done anything. He hasn't tried to talk to me or follow me. And that's the problem: he hasn't done anything, but he's getting to me."

"Nobody likes to be spied on. If you'd like, I'll take him."

"No, thanks. I need to deal with it myself."

The conversation with a colleague took place in line at the cafeteria, and was sparked by Dr. Nesse's sighting of the guy seated once again on the stone bench beneath the mango tree. Dr. Nesse wasn't physically intimidated; he wasn't scared of verbal aggression and he wasn't overwhelmed by his patient's intelligence. But he still couldn't escape the feeling that he was being threatened. When he left the cafeteria after lunch, there the guy was, sitting under the mango tree. And he was still there when the doctor drove down the street that led out of the campus.

The doctor worked mornings at the university hospital in the Urca District, and spent afternoons at his private practice in Ipanema, six blocks from the building where he lived. He always traveled by car from the university to his office and from his office to his house. He didn't like walking. He couldn't stand the busy sidewalks or bumping into people coming toward him; he often hesitated, hoping to avoid a collision, unsure whether to dodge the oncoming pedestrian by moving to the right or the left. But he only faced that dilemma on the rare occasions when he decided to walk from his office to his home.

It was past eight when he finished with his last patient. Even with daylight savings time, it was already dark by the time he reached home. The only person in the living room was Letícia, his older daughter, who was putting her books and notebooks in her backpack. His wife and other daughter were watching TV in the next room.

"Hi, Dad."

"Hi, Letícia."

"One of your patients was here this afternoon. He looked a little lost."

"Did he say his name?"

"No, he just asked if you were here."

"What did he look like?"

"Tall, thin, black hair. He wouldn't be bad looking if it weren't for the stubble."

"What did he say?"

"He asked if this was where Dr. Artur Nesse lived, and if he was home."

"Did he come in?"

"No, he just stayed at the door, looking around."

"Looking at what?"

"Just looking. He looked at me as if taking my picture. Then he thanked me and left; I don't even think he heard me answer."

Dr. Nesse sat looking at his daughter without saying a word.

"You're staring at me the same way."

The doctor moved his head from side to side, as if stretching the muscles in his neck, and left the room. As he was passing through the TV room, he accepted a kiss from his wife and other daughter before going into his bedroom. He only reemerged when his wife called him for dinner.

As soon as they were seated, Dr. Nesse cleared his throat and waited for everyone to give him their attention.

"I want to tell you all something. This afternoon a guy came here looking for me. If he should happen to come back, do not let him come up. If he's already in the hallway, don't open the door. If he doesn't leave, call the doorman. He's tall and thin, with black hair and a stubbly beard. He's a psychotic, a patient from the hospital. Don't let him get near you."

"He didn't do anything, Dad. He was polite, thanked me, and left."

"But he's a psychotic."

"He seemed calm. His eyes looked normal and his voice was pleasant. I couldn't see any signs of illness."

"But he could be dangerous."

The rest of the dinner conversation touched on other subjects. The younger girl remained silent. The only questions his wife asked had to do with the food. She waited to offer her opinion until they were in bed.

"I think Letícia's curiosity is perfectly natural. I'm curious myself. Who is the guy?"

"One of my patients from the hospital."

"Is he really dangerous?"

"Any psychotic patient is potentially dangerous."

"That's a technical answer. Do you really think he could harm any of us?"

"I'm still not sure. I haven't had much contact with him."

"Then why are you so nervous about him? How did he get under your skin?"

"I don't know. He scares me."

"Has he threatened you?"

"No. It's like Letícia said: he's calm and polite, totally unthreatening. At least so far. He just looks. He stares at me the entire day. I don't want him to do the same to you and the girls."

"Maybe he just wants to stare."

"Maybe."

But Dr. Nesse had trouble falling asleep. He got up several times in the night to go to the bathroom. He only managed to doze off in the early-morning hours, after taking a sleeping pill. The next day, he left early: he had a meeting with the director of the hospital, in which he was planning to ask for more rooms and more interns. En route, he reviewed every point he wanted to make. There was plenty of space to build new rooms, and it wouldn't be terribly expensive; the rooms didn't need to be big, and they didn't need any technical equipment. All they required was the standard furniture of psychiatric consultation rooms.

When he arrived on the university campus and turned into the doctors' parking area, he spotted Jonas by the entry gate, chatting with the parking attendant. As he passed them, with his windows up, he saw their mouths move in silent greeting. He parked, locked the car, and went into the building without looking behind himself. As he walked down the hallway toward the conference room, he wondered how the guy knew that he'd be getting in early that morning. He didn't think it was a coincidence. It wasn't a day he received patients, and even if it had been he didn't need to be there at eight in the morning. Jonas must have seen the notice about the meeting on the bulletin board.

Everyone was seated around the conference table when Dr. Nesse arrived. He greeted the director and his colleagues, signed in, and tried to focus on the director's statement about the next year's budget. It cost him great effort to concentrate on the discussion that followed. He found himself staring at two porcelain pharmacist's jars, dating from the Imperial period, that had been used in the old hospital to store medicinal and chemical substances. One of them was labeled, in black letters, TEREB. COSIDA; the other, BALS. OPODELD. In his imagination he returned to a time when doctors employed boiled turpentine and opodeldoc balsam to treat sicknesses of body and soul. His gaze traveled the great jacaranda bookcase that occupied most of the room's biggest wall, lingering on the notches in the columns, before examining the reflections of his colleagues in the glass tabletop. The meeting lasted an hour. When he left the hospital to meet his first patient, he needed to check his notes in order to recall what exactly had been decided about the various items on the list.

Just as he did every day upon leaving home in his car, Dr. Nesse turned onto the first street leading toward Ipanema Beach, where he headed in the direction of Copacabana. He enjoyed driving to the hospital along the seaside, and this Wednesday had begun sunnily, with a cool breeze from the east. He pushed a button inside his car and the voice of Maria Callas filled the sound-proofed interior, which was also protected against the heat and the beggars at the stoplights. He settled into the leather interior and surrendered to his greatest plea-sures: his car and opera, which were really a single joy, since he only listened to opera in the car, alone; he wouldn't be able to stand the sound of another voice, or even the presence of another person, when he was lis-tening to Callas. He also liked Pavarotti. Not because he thought Pavarotti could compare to the diva, but because he thought he kind of looked like the tenor. He was sorry it was such a short drive to the hospital. Under normal traffic conditions, it didn't take more than twenty minutes. The previous Wednesday, he hadn't made any attempt to avoid the bottlenecks; listening to Callas sing *Norma*, he had been grateful for the rain. This week, though, there wouldn't be any impediment, and min-utes before his shift began he entered the campus park-ing lot and had to turn the music off.

He had scheduled Jonas for ten; he reserved eleven o'clock appointments for first-time interviews. At ten on the dot Jonas entered the room. The doctor was shocked to see him without his beard. Not that he devoted much thought to the subject, but because he immediately remembered his daughter's remark that Jonas would be better looking without it. But, he realized, that wasn't precisely what disturbed him: it was the idea that his daughter might have had something to do with the change. Moreover, his sense that he knew Jonas from somewhere was even stronger now that he was beardless. But Jonas had never indicated that they had met before.

"Good morning, Dr. Nesse."

"Good morning, Jonas."

"I'm happy about your choice."

"What do you mean?"

"Your decision to call me Jonas."

"You must have heard it that way."

"What problem do you have with calling me Jonas?"

"It's not my problem, it's yours."

"It's not my problem. I'm happy with Jonas."

"And Isidoro Cruz?"

"That's the name my parents chose."

"Nobody chooses their own name."

"That's why people are so unhappy. If they can't even choose their own names, how can they choose anything else?"

"Do you always think of yourself as Jonas, or are you ever Isidoro?"

"I occasionally have to hear people calling me by a name that isn't my own, but I never feel like Isidoro Cruz. I only answer when people call me Jonas."

"And is that what you're going to do here?"

"You already think of me as Jonas."

"Why do you think that?"

"Because you called me Jonas when I came in, even though you won't admit it. Speaking of which, I bought a bicycle."

"Speaking of what?"

"Of the fact that young people have bicycles."

"What does that have to do with your changing your name?"

"With changing my name, nothing, but it does have something to do with choices."

"And you chose to get a bicycle?"

"That's right. Doesn't your daughter have a bicycle?"

Having two daughters had always worried Dr. Nesse. Not because he had two of them but because they were women. He thought sons were less dependent on fatherly attention, and that they learned early on how to defend themselves from life's dangers. That's how he had been and he assumed that's how it was for all boys. Of course, there were the weak ones, the sickly, the victims of wars and natural disasters. Of all the varieties of handicapped people, though, he'd always been most perturbed by people with mental illnesses. He saw some of them as sorts of defective models; others he considered to have exceptional qualities, as if their handicap had somehow transmuted into an outstanding ability—an ability to do harm, yes, but an outstanding capacity nonetheless. As for this patient, he still didn't know anything about him. Three weeks ago, Jonas had jousted with him with his words; then he'd had the balls to knock on his door and talk to his daughter; and now he'd deployed that reference to the bicycle. The question about the bicycle and the way the session had ended were bothering him. Jonas had been the one to break it off, as if he, and not the doctor, was holding the cards. He couldn't allow these little power games to continue; if he did, he'd be letting the patient take control of the sessions and determine the pace of the treatment.

He had lunch by himself. He didn't feel like discussing the case with anybody and he couldn't think about anything besides Jonas/Isidoro.

The contented feeling he usually experienced upon settling down in his car with the music on was absent that afternoon. He left the hospital a half hour ahead of schedule, without having any plans for that extra time. While he was driving, rather than having his spirit filled with the voice of Maria Callas, he was invaded by scenes of the encounter between his daughter and his young patient. It was not a mere coincidence that he had shaved his beard, no more casual than his references to buying a bicycle and his daughter. Coincidences like that didn't happen. They were clear signs that he and Letícia were seeing each other on the sly.

Only when he was parking did he realize that he had driven home rather than to his office. He parked in the garage and went up. When he opened the door, he was received by a disquieting silence. The maid appeared in the living room.

"Is something the matter, Doctor?"

"No. Nothing. Where is everyone?"

"They went out."

"Did anyone come here looking for me?"

"No, sir."

"Or looking for the girls?"

"No."

"Nobody called?"

"No, sir."

The bicycle had been sitting in the parking garage for more than a year without ever seeming to be used. Jonas had seen it thousands of times, but he'd only had the idea to buy it after he noticed Dr. Nesse's daughter riding a bike through Ipanema. The one in his garage was one of a pair, attached with a chain. They were both of the same make, one for a man and the other for a woman. The doorman told him that the couple had broken up and that the woman was still living in the building. The bikes were left over from the marriage. He rang the doorbell and asked if she was interested in getting rid of one of the bicycles that were wasting away in the garage. The woman seemed so relieved to see it go that she quickly let him have it, practically free of charge. After cleaning and oiling it, all he had to do was fill the tires.

At the end of the afternoon, Jonas tried out his new vehicle at the same time Letícia was leaving her apartment. A chat with the doorman revealed that she usually left home on her bike in order to go to the gym, every day at the end of the afternoon, as long as it wasn't raining. He didn't wait for her in front of the building, but on the corner of the next block; and he made the encounter seem perfectly accidental, helped along by a near traffic jam of bicycles, common on busy Ipanema corners. Letícia took a few seconds to recognize the guy who'd been by her apartment.

"You shaved your beard!"

"Do you like it?"

"Sure, of course, it's that . . . when I met you I kept thinking how much better you'd look without a beard, and now you've shaved it. It freaks me out a little."

"In a good way?"

"Yeah. Do you live in Ipanema too?"

"I do. Over near the Praça General Osório."

"I still don't know your name."

"Jonas. And yours?"

"Letícia."

"Nice name."

They rode together to the gym, about six blocks away. Conversation was prevented by the passing cars and buses and had to be taken up again at the door to the gym. Two hours later, in front of Letícia's building, the conversation came to a halt again. She hadn't fit in any exercise. They had talked about where they liked to hang out, what films they'd seen, and what books they'd read, things they liked and disliked.

Two days had passed since the last session, and that morning Dr. Nesse still hadn't run into his patient at the hospital. He wasn't on the bench under the mango tree and he wasn't in the recreation room; he didn't see him at lunchtime, crossing the patio on the way to the cafeteria. Perhaps he had grown tired of playing stalker.

The doctor ate in peace, got in the car he'd parked in the shade of a big tree, and headed for the office.

The moment he heard Callas's voice come through the stereo, he fell into a state of well-being, a thing that had been becoming increasingly rare in his life. It wasn't an especially nice day, which made no difference, as long as the sound of *Norma* occupied every square inch of his car's interior. His only concern was steeling himself so he didn't close his eyes when her voice peaked. He was brusquely interrupted from his moment of rapture. It took him a while to focus on the gestures of the cyclist who was moving alongside his car. He looked like he was waving good-bye to someone.

He didn't recognize the rider at first. The bike was weaving between two lanes of traffic, and the doctor had to maneuver carefully to avoid slamming the cyclist against the car in the next lane. Only when the man continued to wave did he realize that it was Jonas. The car swerved slightly to the right, then returned to the lane, while the cyclist slowed down and hung back. Dr. Nesse checked to make sure everything was all right and turned off the stereo. He looked in the rearview mirror, but he didn't see the cyclist. He checked the sidewalks, looked ahead of him on the street, and into the rearview mirror again, but there was no sign of Jonas.

The encounter took place on the Avenida Atlântica, near the Praça do Lido. The traffic was flowing regularly, even though there were quite a lot of cars out. Dr. Nesse kept moving ahead, looking repeatedly to the sides and into the rearview mirror. Before he'd gotten halfway down Copacabana Beach, he began to have his doubts. It might have been just another bicycler waving at someone on the sidewalk. Since he'd been thinking about Jonas so much in the last few days, it was perfectly possible that he could have mixed him up with a guy on a bike, especially since he'd said he'd bought a bicycle. But he couldn't deny that he'd had a very good look at him. Their eyes had met from a distance of only a couple of feet. There was no way he could be mistaken. When he turned toward Ipanema at the end of the beach, his hands were sweating in spite of the air-conditioning. Instead of going to the office, he went home, as he'd done two days ago. Letícia was there.

"Hi, Dad! Home at this hour?"

"Hi . . ."

"You're pale. Are you feeling okay?"

"No. It must have been the heat."

"Could be. Do you want me to call Mom?"

"No. Everything's fine. That guy who was here looking for me . . . did he ever show up again?"

"Not here at the house."

"Anywhere else?"

"I ran into him on the street, on a bike."

"Now?"

"No, a couple of days ago, when I was going to the gym. Our bikes almost bumped into each other. If he hadn't stopped, I wouldn't have recognized him. He'd shaved . . . he was a lot cuter."

"Letícia, he's my patient."

"Nothing happened, Dad, we just chatted for a little bit. It was just one of those things. We hadn't planned it."

"You didn't plan it, but he could have orchestrated it."

"And how was he going to know exactly what time I was going to be on my bike on that corner? The guy's nice and polite. What's going on, Dad? What did he do?"

"Nothing."

Dr. Nesse was covered with sweat. He took a quick shower, changed clothes, and went to his office.

Jonas had fallen into the habit of going to the hospital every morning. The first few times, he'd felt uncomfortable around the inpatients. He wasn't scared of them—for the most part they seemed inoffensive, or at least less offensive than regular people—but those first few mornings he was completely focused on Dr. Nesse.

Only after he'd figured out the doctor's routine, which was inflexible, had he begun meeting the gazes and greetings of the patients with whom he shared the court-yard. Depending on how heavily medicated they were, their voices were strange and they tended to speak in clichés, but they still managed to establish a modicum of contact. What Jonas found most disconcerting wasn't their words but the smell of disinfectant that clung to their clothes. That's why he preferred seeing them on the outdoor patio, by the trees, rather than in enclosed locations. Except on the days he had his appointments, he avoided meeting Dr. Nesse around the hospital; he only let himself be seen in the distance or greeted him when he arrived in his car, with his windows closed.

Jonas had been noting small changes in the doctor. Physical changes, more than verbal ones: a different way of walking, fewer spontaneous gestures, a state of corporeal alertness, as if he felt himself to be in danger. The doctor no doubt couldn't specify the nature of the danger, couldn't even say if the danger was real; from his point of view there was nothing for it but to keep on with his routine exactly as before. The climate in his treatment sessions had changed at a precise moment, Jonas thought: when he'd mentioned the doctor's daughter. He wondered if Dr. Nesse had learned about his meeting with Letícia. But he didn't think there was anything to be afraid of. After all, nobody had done anything to anyone.

Letícia had started riding her bike more often than usual, even when she had nothing else to do outside besides reflect on her encounter with Jonas. She didn't know what was happening. The impression her father gave was that she and the rest of the family were in terrible danger, a danger that only a medical eye could detect. But what could that eye reveal? She couldn't begin to fathom it.

While she was pedaling around, watching the traffic, she was also checking out the other cyclists. She didn't expect to run into him on Saturday morning, though their first encounter had also been unexpected.

Letícia herself was planning to study medicine, but she wasn't interested in psychiatry. She didn't like the way her father viewed people and she didn't like the principles he had tried to instill in her and her sister: she thought there was a considerable distance between psychiatry (or maybe just the way her dad practiced it) and the modern world. But above all she didn't want to dedicate her life to crazy people. She preferred medicine with more visible practical results. She also didn't think her father's professional background had given him any deeper understanding of the people around him. Her mother had long since submitted to her husband's will.

To avoid the intense traffic in Ipanema, she'd decided to make a circle around the Lagoa Rodrigo de Freitas bike path, which would make an impromptu encounter with Jonas unlikely. What would her father say if he knew that their meeting hadn't been as brief as she'd told him? How would he react if he learned that instead of going to the gym she'd sat talking to Jonas for two hours? And that he'd accompanied her to the door of their building, and that they'd agreed to meet again, and that she found him attractive? Such thoughts consumed her on the eight kilometers around the lake.

On Sunday mornings, she thought, people take their bikes along the beach. If the next day turned out to be pretty, there was a greater chance of bumping into Jonas—and the weather seemed stable. She'd put on a bikini under her clothes, in case they decided to go swimming. They'd leave their bikes chained together on the sand and they'd have the whole Sunday to get to know each other. They wouldn't even need to go anywhere to eat, since the vendors would sell them anything they wanted right on the beach, from sandwiches to pizzas to cold beer. They'd watch the sunset over Ipanema, Gávea Rock, the silhouette of the Two Brothers, the sea changing colors, from green to golden. They wouldn't leave until after dark.

She'd be there the next day, and what she most desired was for Jonas to be there too.

Jonas didn't see any reason to go to the hospital on Saturday. First, because Dr. Nesse wouldn't be there and the place would be full of patients' relatives. But the main reason had to do with Letícia. There was a possibility of meeting her on her bike on Saturday as well as Sunday, though he thought Sunday was more likely, as that was when the beachfront boulevards were blocked to automobile traffic.

He didn't know if Dr. Nesse had told his daughter anything about him, but he might have at least suggested that his elevator didn't go all the way to the top floor, that he claimed a different name than the one on his ID, and he might have pegged a clinical diagnosis on him, and Letícia might have asked if it was anything serious, and he would have said yes, and she would think about it a lot and eventually decide that it didn't matter, that Jonas was a good guy, that her dad didn't understand the younger generation, that he didn't even understand her, so how could he understand a complete stranger?

That afternoon, he took his bike along the beachfront, from the top of Copacabana to the end of Leblon, a kind of scouting sortie in preparation for the next day. The sea was churning, and the waves were high. Only surfers dared to venture into the water, and only a very few had come out with their surfboards. The waves broke with such violence that he could feel the ground shake. He headed back home at the end of the afternoon, after perusing the terrain twice and selecting the best parts of the beach for their purposes. Before he even reached his street, he felt the first raindrops. He looked up. The sky was full of lead-gray clouds. As he entered the garage of his building, the rain burst through the clouds.

It rained the whole of Saturday night and all Sunday morning. It was three in the afternoon when Jonas got his bike and headed toward Letícia's building. The streets were still wet and he had to move slowly in order not to get dirty water all over his pants. He still didn't know how he'd announce his arrival without Dr. Nesse or anyone else in the house noticing. He wasn't even certain she'd be home. It was Sunday; she might be out. As he passed a corner with a public phone, he made a U-turn, hopped off the bike seat, and dialed the number he knew by heart.

"I'd like to speak with Dr. Nesse, please."

"Dr. Nesse has gone to answer a call. Would you like to leave your name and number? He'll call you as soon as he gets back."

"Thanks. I'll try back later."

It wasn't Letícia's voice. From the tone, he was sure it wasn't the maid, either, and it wasn't a girl: it could only have been the doctor's wife. He traveled the remaining two blocks, checked to make sure his clothes were free of mud, went into the building's lobby, and spoke to the doorman.

"Could you call up to Letícia, in 501, please?"

After a few minutes, once Jonas had stored his bicycle in the garage, the two left on foot.

"I was hoping to run into you on your bike this morning, if it hadn't been raining."

"I thought the same thing . . . I didn't even have your phone number to change plans."

"I've got your number, but I thought your father would get upset if I called."

"He sure would have."

"Maybe someday he'll change his mind about me."

"Why doesn't he like you?"

"I don't think it's that he likes or dislikes me, but I'm a patient of his. . . . It's a principle of medicine, not to get your clinical cases mixed up with your private life."

"And why are you a clinical case?"

"I'm not exactly a clinical case. I'm just someone who sought help from a service offered by the university."

"And why was that?"

"It's an old story. . . . Someday we'll talk about it."

A weekend free of Jonas allowed Dr. Nesse to enter the hospital on Monday morning with a certain hope that his patient might have decided to abandon his siege. He wasn't at the parking lot entrance, or sitting on the bench under the mango tree. But he might be in the recreation room, or maybe he was late, or he might have even stayed home. After all, he didn't work at the hospital; he didn't need to explain to anyone what he was or wasn't doing there. Dr. Nesse wouldn't be seeing Jonas until Wednesday, and it was only Monday. It was always possible, even on days he didn't have appointments, that he'd be loitering in the courtyard. Just in case, Dr. Nesse worked with his blinds partly open. Every once in a while he glanced up to make sure the bench was still empty. The bench must still be wet from the weekend rain; the morning sun was not enough to dry the stone. Jonas could be somewhere else on the grounds, or even inside the building. In the middle of the morning, when he left his office to get a cup of coffee, he asked the doormen if they'd seen a certain patient, giving a quick description.

"We know Jonas, Doctor. He didn't come today."

He asked his receptionist to call the patient Isidoro Cruz, or Jonas, and see if he was home. She tried a few times, but nobody answered.

"Please call my house."

As she was dialing, the doctor returned to examine the courtyard. This time, he didn't hide behind the blinds.

"Doctor, the maid said everyone left."

"Call her back and ask if anyone left with them."

While the receptionist was calling, the doctor never took his eyes off the window.

"Doctor, the maid said that they all left at different times and that she doesn't know if any of them left with anyone else."

"What do you mean, she doesn't know?"

"She's still on the line, Doctor. Maybe you might want to ask her yourself."

"Hello . . ."

"It's me, Doctor. Aparecida."

"Aparecida, did a guy come looking for me or Letícia?"

"No, sir, at least not here at the door."

"Don't open the door to any strangers, okay?"

"Yes, sir."

The two patients who followed this conversation suffered for it. There was no way for him to listen to them talk and still keep an eye on the stone bench beneath the mango tree. After lunch, Dr. Nesse didn't drive directly to the office. He needed to go by his apartment to make sure everything was all right. It wouldn't take ten minutes. But he didn't even need to go up: the doorman told him that his wife and younger daughter were there. Letícia was still out. He returned to his car, certain that there was no reason to go up. His wife wouldn't know where Letícia was. And her sister, even if she knew, wouldn't say anything. He got into the car and headed to the office.

His secretary had turned on the air-conditioning an hour before he got there, to ensure that the temperature would be pleasant when he started receiving patients. The room was agreeable and tastefully decorated. He had hired an architect for that purpose, a male architect: he'd feared that a woman would create a space that was less masculine, less austere. The chair and the couch were of Italian design and upholstered in black leather (as he thought appropriate to a man's office). No colonial furniture, no Indian textiles.

His secretary reviewed the afternoon's schedule with him and handed him the receipts from the payments and bank deposits she'd made that morning. The doctor barely paid attention. He stuffed the receipts in his pocket and went into his office.

He sat there in the half-light, with the blinds closed. While he waited for his first patient, he reviewed the recent episodes with Jonas. He decided that the first thing he had to do was decide whether to keep seeing Jonas or to send him to another colleague. If he decided to continue seeing him, he couldn't allow his fantasies to keep interfering with his treatment. If they were fantasies. It wasn't a fantasy that Jonas had gone to his apartment and talked to his daughter, and it wasn't a fantasy that he'd met her when she was riding her bike; he hadn't imagined Jonas's revelation that he'd bought a bicycle or his allusion to the doctor's daughter's bicycle; and it was a fact that Jonas spent every morning seated on the bench in the courtyard watching the doctor's every move. He made up his mind to use the next session to propose certain limits in the psychiatric treatment, and the most important boundary he would establish was that the patient was not to involve himself in the doctor's private or family life. If Jonas accepted those limits, they could continue the treatment. If he resisted, the treatment would be terminated.

It was at least a way to regain control of the situation, instead of simply reacting to the patient. He didn't agree with those who believed that patients could be treated only with words; some needed medication. It was too early to know just what mental problems Jonas had, but he certainly couldn't expose his daughter to Jonas's sickness. At the end of the day, he left the office feeling much better than when he'd arrived. In the car, he put on the Maria Callas CD and was happy to note that his soul was once again ready to hear it. He allowed himself to hum a few bars in a duet with the diva.

Tuesday passed the way he would have liked every weekday to pass. Not even the prospect of seeing Jonas the next day could disrupt the peace he felt. Everything went smoothly, morning and afternoon, and there was no sign of Jonas/Isidoro.

He awoke the next day even more buoyant than the night before. He sat down alone at the breakfast table; the girls had already left and his wife was still asleep. He didn't like company at breakfast; he preferred to read the paper without interruptions. He set aside the sports section, which didn't interest him, scanned the pages dedicated to domestic and international politics, and perused the second section more carefully, regretting that there was little or no space devoted to opera.

He left home fifteen minutes earlier than usual, turned onto the cross street that led to Ipanema Beach, took a left on the beachfront avenue, and headed for the hospital. Since he had plenty of time, he decided to let himself go with the flow of the traffic, taking time to watch the people running or walking on the sidewalk next to the beach. He thought he ought to do the same at least three times a week, to try to lose weight. Even though he was tall, he could still stand to lose twenty pounds. But the mere idea of putting on shorts, a T-shirt, and tennis shoes and venturing outside in the summer sun was enough to make his knees go weak. He checked the air-conditioning and forgot about the morning athletes. The traffic moved slowly but continuously, so regularly that he hardly needed to pay attention. Soon he was steering the car through the iron gates of the hospital.

At ten sharp he opened the door to the waiting room in order to let Jonas in. There was nobody in the waiting room. He closed the door and used the internal phone to speak to the psychiatric sector's main receptionist.

"The patient for ten o'clock hasn't arrived yet, Doctor."

"You know who he is . . ."

"Jonas is always around, Doctor. As soon as he gets here, I'll send him up."

Ten minutes later, the doctor was sure that Jonas wouldn't be coming. He paced the room, opened the door, checked the waiting room a few more times, consulted the attendant again, and felt the inner peace he had enjoyed so much over the last couple of days disappear.

At lunchtime, en route to the cafeteria, he stopped by the recreation room and the occupational therapy center, then walked through the courtyard, checking all the places where Jonas was usually on guard. No sign.

On Thursday morning, Jonas parked his bike in the courtyard beside the mango tree and headed to the guard booth to greet the employees.

"The doctor asked about you yesterday."

"Yesterday I couldn't come."

At twelve sharp, after seeing his morning patients, Dr. Nesse passed the guard booth on his way to the cafeteria. Crossing the courtyard, he slowed as if preparing to stop and even began to turn left, toward the stone bench where Jonas was sitting, but he resisted the temptation. He continued straight on to lunch.

When he returned to his room to pick up his briefcase, he found an urgent message on his desk asking him to call home immediately. He'd gone out in the morning without realizing that Letícia hadn't come home the night before. She still wasn't back and nobody knew where she was.

He hung up the phone and ran out to the courtyard. Jonas was no longer there.

Letícia had told her mother that she was going to spend two nights with a girlfriend, studying for their exams. It was common enough, right before exams, for a few girls to get together at one of their homes to study, and for them to sleep over. What wasn't so common was for one of the girls from the study group to call at night and ask for Letícia. Her mother assumed at first that it was a mistake, rather than that their daughter had lied. To make sure, she'd called one of the other girls in the group, who not only didn't know where Letícia was but informed her that they had made no plans to study with her that night.

All Wednesday night, Teresa Nesse had kept their daughter's absence a secret. She'd seen her husband get up the next morning and ask their other daughter where her sister was. Teresa's doubts and anxiety increased throughout the morning. At exactly noon, which was the limit she'd set herself, she called her husband at the university to inform him that Letícia had disappeared.

Dr. Nesse received the envelope as soon as he walked through the hospital reception area, right after he'd hung up with his wife. On the envelope the words DR. NESSE were printed in block letters. Inside was half a sheet of standard office paper with the phrase "How are you doing?" written in a slightly shaking hand.

"Who gave you this envelope?"

"A boy. He said it was for you."

"What kind of boy? What did he look like?"

"He looked like a street kid, Doctor. Shorts, sandals, T-shirt."

"How long ago was this?"

"Just a minute ago; you were at lunch."

The doctor ran out into the courtyard, up to the gate, looking in vain for a boy matching the receptionist's description. But he didn't even know what the boy would look like.

He walked into his apartment a half hour later, asking about his daughter as he held out the note to his wife.

"What is this, Artur? Does it have something to do with Letícia?"

"He's kidnapped Letícia."

"Who kidnapped Letícia, Artur? Jesus Christ, what are you talking about? Where's my daughter?" Tears were streaming down her face and her lips were trembling so much she could barely get the words out.

"I'm saying that he kidnapped our daughter."

"That guy? Your patient?"

"Right."

"How do you know it was him?"

"I just know it."

"Did you see the two of them together?"

"No, but he came to the hospital today and sat on that bench looking at me."

"So, Artur . . . if he was at the hospital, he couldn't have been with Letícia."

"I still didn't know that Letícia had disappeared."

"Artur, this doesn't make any sense! If the guy was with her, he wouldn't go to the hospital just to stare at you."

"He's crazy! I warned you!"

"But if he kidnapped Letícia, what was he doing at the hospital?"

"Looking."

"Looking at what?"

"Looking at me, what the fuck else?"

"Calm down, Artur. I'm scared. I don't get any of this. How can a man who kidnapped our daughter spend the morning sitting in the courtyard of the hospital?"

"I have his chart, with his phone number, address, everything. I'm going to go get that son of a bitch."

"Don't you think we ought to go to the police? You have that note . . ."

Dr. Nesse didn't believe in disappearances or in kidnapping, even though he'd been the first to use that word. Running off, or being taken away: those words fit better. His daughter had been taken away. Worse yet, she had done so with a patient of his. Even though he had no proof that she'd been taken away, he didn't doubt that that was what had happened. And the fact was, his daughter had been missing for more than twenty-four hours. If he was right, Jonas would be missing too.

He reached into his pocket and retrieved the paper on which he'd scrawled Jonas's number and address. He called immediately. The phone rang more than ten times. Nobody answered. He tried a few more times: no answer. Not even a machine. He was sure Jonas and Letícia were together. He had to find out where.

According to the maid, Letícia had left the house carrying only a bag, big enough to contain no more than a change of clothes and a few personal items. Dr. Nesse thought about going to motels in search of his daughter, but then realized the idea was absurd. They could be in the house of some friend whose parents were out of town. He had his wife call Letícia's friends, in the hope of finding something out. He thought his wife should have kept a closer watch on their daughter, and blamed her somewhat for her disappearance. The calls turned up nothing. Her friends hadn't seen Letícia for two days and they'd never heard her mention Jonas or any new boyfriend.

At two in the afternoon, Dr. Nesse got into his car, having decided to drive through all of Copacabana, Ipanema, and Leblon. For some reason, he didn't think his daughter would have left those neighborhoods and he hoped to find the two of them riding their bikes through the streets. At the end of the day he stopped by the hospital to see if Jonas had returned in the afternoon. No such luck.

Back in his car, driving up and down the streets, he decided that his daughter wouldn't spend more than one more night away from home. The doctor didn't think they'd eloped. They didn't live in some backwoods village, they lived in Rio de Janeiro, in the neighborhood of Ipanema, and it was the twenty-first century. No modern teenager would feel the need to run off in order to consummate a sexual relationship.

There was still the possibility of a kidnapping, for the same reason: they lived in Ipanema, in Rio de Janeiro. At least when people eloped it was consensual, whereas kidnapping implied brute force and the danger of death.

He thought about going to the police. The idea, which he'd rejected a few hours before, started to seem like a viable option. He didn't trust the police, but he remembered the praises one of his colleagues at the hospital had heaped on an officer in Copacabana, who had dealt with a case involving a patient. He'd remembered the cop's name because it was the name of a philosopher. He kept driving without knowing exactly where to. He realized, though, that he was heading toward Ipanema.

And what if Jonas's decision to seek treatment was just part of a plan to kidnap one of his daughters? And what if all that story about wanting to be called Jonas and not Isidoro was just a farce? Maybe he wasn't named Jonas or Isidoro. Maybe he'd given him a fake phone number. He reached into his pocket and got out the paper again. There was the address: Rua Jangadeiros. He knew it was near the Praça General Osório, right by his office. They were neighbors. He imagined Jonas sitting in the square, observing him as he entered and left the building. . . . He imagined Jonas seeing his elegant car and thinking that he was rich. . . . He might have come up with a plan to present himself as a psychiatric patient in order to get free treatment in the hospital and have easy access to the doctor, without seeming suspicious. The visit to his apartment, the casual meeting with Letícia, everything fit: psychotic Jonas was a brilliant disguise for an intelligent, cold, meticulous kidnapper who had planned everything carefully, step by step, including the idea of making Letícia fall in love with him. He didn't even have to kidnap her; she'd probably just followed him.

He parked in the garage of his office. Jonas's street wasn't a hundred yards away. He walked to the corner and looked for the number he'd copied from the file. The street was only two blocks long; he walked it up and down, on both sides. He couldn't find the number Jonas had given.

⏤

The conversation with the chief was made possible only thanks to the intervention of an on-duty officer who'd observed the comings and goings of a toweringly tall man on the sidewalk in front of the building. Dr. Nesse had never in his life been inside a police station, and he had never imagined that he would one day be inside one to report his daughter's disappearance.

"Sir, do you need help?"

"I do. Are you the chief?"

"I'm a detective. If you'd like to speak with the chief . . ."

"I don't know . . . maybe it's better . . ."

Even while he was speaking to the officer, Dr. Nesse didn't stop pacing, two steps forward, two steps back, fidgeting in his pockets, looking for something—he didn't know what—and then folding and unfolding a piece of paper he'd found in his pants pocket.

"Maybe you'd better come in, sir."

The detective took Dr. Nesse into the building. As they were taking the steps up to the second floor, the doctor thought about backing out, but the detective's hand on his shoulder encouraged him to continue. When they entered the chief's office, he was deep in discussion with another officer. He didn't even raise his eyes when the detective entered the room with a man who was wiping his nose with a crumpled handkerchief. They stood there for two long minutes before the chief focused on them.

"What is it, Ramos?"

"I think this gentleman has some kind of problem, sir."

"Did he say what the problem was?"

"He's nervous, sir, he can't quite say what happened."

The chief sent the other subordinate away and looked at Dr. Nesse for the first time.

"What happened?" There was fatigue and impatience in the man's voice.

"Are you Chief Espinosa?"

"Chief Espinosa is on holiday. I'm the deputy. Is he the one you have to see?"

"I don't know. . . . He's the one I know."

"You don't want to tell me what happened?"

"My daughter . . . disappeared. . . . Maybe kidnapped."

"Ramos, bring him a cup of water."

After gulping down the water, the doctor introduced himself and gave a short, monotone description of his daughter's disappearance. By the time he was done, he seemed more composed, and his voice had recovered its normal sound.

"It's not kidnapping when the victim goes off with the supposed kidnapper of her own free will."

"Sorry, sir, but you can't speak of free will when it comes to a minor. She was seduced by an older, more experienced man."

"Even so, it's not kidnapping. How old is she?"

"Seventeen."

"Was there any contact? Ransom notes?"

The doctor removed from his pocket the envelope with the note and handed it to the officer.

"Just this."

"When did you get it?"

"Today, around noon."

"How was it delivered?"

"A boy left it in the lobby of the hospital where I work."

"The handwriting is disguised."

"That was hardly necessary. I know who wrote it."

"You do?"

"Yes."

"Who?"

"A patient."

"Then we'll have to call him in."

"I can't."

"Why not?"

"He's a patient."

"But, Doctor . . ."

"I can't."

"What is your specialty?"

"Psychiatry."

"So your patient is crazy?"

"I can't guarantee that he's psychotic. He could have made it all up."

"Why are you so worried about medical ethics, if he might be a fraud?"

"That doesn't matter to us."

"Listen, Doctor. You came here to report the alleged kidnapping of your daughter; you show us a note that doesn't prove anything, but that you believe to be from the kidnapper; you say you know who it is, but then say you can't reveal his name. How does that sound to you? The note is not only vague, it's just a question—it doesn't have your name on it or your daughter's and makes no reference to a kidnapping. Maybe they ran off together. If you insist on keeping your patient's name a secret, the only thing we can do is hope that that was the case."

"You can't start an investigation with the information I've already given?"

"What would we investigate? The note says nothing, it's not even a note; there's nothing connecting it to the disappearance of your daughter, except the date. And one more thing: it's very suspicious that your daughter told your wife she was going to sleep over at a friend's house on the exact same day she disappeared. Nobody gives a warning that they're going to be kidnapped. It's a typical lie from a girl who's going to sleep with her boyfriend. I'd be willing to bet that your daughter will come home within a day or two begging forgiveness and crying that she was lied to."

"Which she certainly was."

"Wait until tomorrow, Doctor. If your daughter hasn't shown up by then, I promise you we'll find her. Think about it: up until now, nothing's happened. How many times has your daughter slept over with friends?"

"A few."

"Are you sure that she was really with her friends every time?"

"I don't know."

"Call me and report back tomorrow."

"Could you also give me Chief Espinosa's phone number? I'd like to speak to him as well."

⤙

The doctor left the station thinking he'd been right not to want to get involved with the police. They were all insensitive and bureaucratic. If an event didn't fit into one of their preconceived notions, then it wasn't even an event or, worse, it had never happened at all.

He'd left his cell phone in his car, which he'd parked in an underground garage a block from the station. He got the car and drove down the Rua Siqueira Campos to the Avenida Atlântica. He wanted to find a parking place outside where he could stop and call the number the officer had given him.

It wasn't hard to find a spot. It was after seven when he called for the first time. He was hoping to erase the bad impression he'd got from the deputy. But he still didn't know how the real chief would respond.

"Chief Espinosa?"

"Yes."

"I'm sorry to be calling you at home, but at the station they said you were on vacation."

"That's true."

"My name is Artur Nesse. I'm a doctor. . . . A colleague at the hospital gave me your name. . . . You helped him . . ."

Despite the officer's initial resistance, he finally agreed to meet the doctor in the square in the Peixoto District. Dr. Nesse was only five minutes away, but since he'd lied, saying he was leaving his office in Ipanema, he needed to wait about ten minutes before turning right on the first street ahead of him and heading over to the officer's house.

He drove around the square before settling into a safe place almost directly in front of the building whose address he had noted. As he walked toward the building, a man standing on the sidewalk called his name.

"Dr. Nesse? I'm Chief Espinosa."

They shook hands, and the policeman pointed toward the square.

"Do you mind having our chat outside?"

"No, of course not . . ."

They crossed the street and found a bench where they

wouldn't be disturbed. Neither spoke until they were seated.

"So, Doctor, what happened?"

It was a little after four in the afternoon when Jonas and Letícia arrived, sweating and exhausted, at the door of the house at the very top of the hillside. The sun was still high and they could have dealt with the heat if they had taken the van that ferried passengers up to the top of the hill instead of walking. They rested a few minutes before attacking the stone staircase that led from the street, past the garden terraces, up to the porch of the house.

The Rua Saint Roman was an arch-shaped hillside street on the south flank of Cantagalo Hill, on the border between the neighborhoods of Ipanema and Copacabana. The street still contained a few mansions from the time when rich people preferred the beautiful views of the Atlantic Ocean to the frenetic action of Copacabana, directly below. That was in the time before the favelas had conquered the hilltop; eventually, the humble dwellings directly abutted the back walls of the great houses. With the passage of time, the street lost its cachet and the richer people abandoned it for safer places. Some of the old houses were occupied by new residents, who were more attracted to the quality of the construction than they were put off by the neighborhood. Some of the other houses were transformed into religious institutions. The favela had spontaneously and peacefully stopped growing just behind the old houses, allowing both groups of inhabitants to coexist.

"I sure won't need to go to the gym today, but I'll need a shower when we get up there."

"You'll get your shower, and I promise you'll enjoy it."

The stone house, two stories tall, was separated from the street by a steep garden, divided into little terraces connected by a walkway in the same gray stone that covered the whole facade of the house. There was no doorbell, either on the gate or on the door that opened onto a wide porch in front of the building. The well-tended garden aside, there was nothing to indicate that the house was inhabited: nobody was around, none of the windows were open, there were no chairs on the porch.

When they reached the house, Letícia sat on the little wall that divided the garden from the porch, with her back to the house. In front of her, above the buildings of Copacabana, was a broad swath of blue sea. Jonas lifted the top off a lantern over the main door, removed a key from it, and sat down beside Letícia. They were silent, taking in the view and listening to the babble that rose from the city below like a sonorous cloud.

"You're sure nobody's home?"

"I already checked the other doors and windows. They're closed. Besides, my friend the pastor said he only comes here on weekends for services."

"He's got a house this big but he only uses it on the weekends?"

"It's not his. The owner passed away; he's only the caretaker."

"And what kind of services does he perform?"

"I'm not sure how it started. I think he got interested in some Oriental religions or eastern European religions, I'm not sure—he spent time there, and when he came back he started a kind of branch office here in Rio. I'm not even sure what the name of their religion is. He's been doing it for about two or three years here in this house. When everybody comes, it's more than a hundred people. The church is really poor, and it only survives because of the donations of the faithful."

"You mean, *he* survives on the donations of the faithful."

"*He* is the church."

"And he's your friend."

"I helped him when he came back from Europe. He didn't have money or followers. We shared a room in a boardinghouse on the Rua Cândido Mendes. Until the opportunity came to take care of this house while the estate was being settled. But the estate moved very slowly. While it's still being worked out, he uses the house as a kind of church. That's why there's no sign or symbol outside."

"Can we go in?"

They got their bags, with their clothes and toiletries. Jonas opened the massive wooden door and they went in. The first thing they noticed was the difference in temperature; it was much more pleasant inside the house.

The sun filtered through the blinds; their rustling bags made the silence seem even more striking.

They were in the main living room. Letícia tried the light switch, but nothing happened; she tried another one, which didn't work either. Jonas went into the kitchen, found the switchboard, and turned the electricity on. He heard the hum of the refrigerator coming to life and Letícia's voice, telling him that the lights had come on. At that point they could take a more thorough look at their surroundings. Aside from a few chairs in clashing styles and a hat rack holding a single umbrella, there was nothing else of interest. An archway in the main room led to a small room that seemed to serve as an altar. Inside, a small table was covered with an embroidered cloth and placed against a painting of an actual altar. Everything was very crude and improvised. Besides the little room, there was nothing else in the house indicating that it was connected to any sort of religious activity.

Upstairs were three bedrooms. In what was probably the master bedroom, facing the sea, there was a double bed, a dressing table from which one of the drawers was missing, and a chair. In the dresser drawers were towels and sheets. The bathroom was big, with English fixtures and a large tub. But the peculiar thing about the bathroom was the shower. There was no glass door or curtain, only a half-wall marking the space for the shower. The space was big enough to accommodate three or four people.

Letícia tried out the bathtub faucet. The water flowed

a little brownish at first, but it immediately cleared and warmed up, as if the boiler had been turned on.

"The water's warm."

"The sun must have heated up the tank today. Do you want to bathe now?"

"Yes."

"I'll go downstairs and lock the door and come back to help you."

"I'm not going to take a bath, I'm just going to shower."

"Fine. I'll take one after you're done."

The idea of spending the night together had been Jonas's, the choice of locale his too, but the final decision was made by Letícia, after spending Sunday night remembering everything Jonas had said on Sunday. If Jonas was crazy, she thought, then most people in the world, and most of the best people, were also crazy. She left the door and the window in the bathroom open, to take advantage of the late-afternoon breeze and light, and also in order to think about what was to come. She hadn't remained a virgin until her seventeenth year out of religious principles, out of obedience to her father's moralism, or in order to save herself for Prince Charming. She'd kept her virginity because she was scared. She wasn't religious, she didn't like preachy people, and she didn't believe in Prince Charmings. She told herself that it wasn't fear, it was prudence, but she knew very well that those feelings went hand in hand. She'd also wondered how much of her parents' religiosity and morality she'd unwillingly inherited. And now she saw Jonas coming up the stairs, finding the bathroom door open, and hesitantly coming in. She wondered what he would do next, and how she would react. The water ran down her hair, blurring her vision. Letícia ran her hand across her face, and when her vision was clear again she could make out Jonas in the middle of the bathroom, facing her. He came into the shower and put his arms around her. Slowly, they began to soap each other up, every part of each other's body, every curve, every surface, every bend, every orifice, every protuberance. When every part had been touched and examined, they moved to the bedroom, joined as if dancing, still wet, and stretched out on the bed without allowing their bodies to separate; and that is how they remained until it got dark.

"You didn't tell me you were a virgin. You should have said something."

"What difference would it have made?"

"I'd have been more careful."

"You were careful . . . as if you knew."

"Do you feel anything? Does anything hurt?"

"Only my stomach . . ."

"Your stomach?"

". . . which is starving."

Jonas went to the kitchen to get the sandwiches, the fruit, and the soft drinks they'd brought along. They ate in bed, facing the window, looking at the sky above Copacabana.

"Tomorrow I'll have to go out and buy more food."

"I'm scared to stay here by myself."

"You don't have to be scared—it's safe here. I'll only be gone for a minute. You can't go back home hungry. Don't forget that you're spending two days at a girlfriend's house and you're being well treated."

"I sure am."

One end of the Rua Saint Roman emptied out only two blocks away from the Rua Jangadeiros and the Praça General Osório. On Thursday morning, Jonas exited via that end to retrieve his bike. On his way to the hospital, he avoided Dr. Nesse's usual route. He didn't think it was the right moment for a meeting outside the precincts of the hospital. He had no idea how the doctor would react. It was eleven-thirty when he biked past the gate and greeted the employee who watched the parking lot. Even without entering the reserved area, he could see the doctor's car. He sat on the bench beneath the mango tree and waited.

His attempts to get to know a few of the inpatients, though slow, were starting to pay off. He was already recognized and known by name. They asked him for a soft drink or a packet of cookies, and he did what he could when he could. He didn't want to make his goodwill gestures feel obligatory. Whoever saw him, day after day, seated on his bench, talking to the patients,

participating in the recreational activities and occupational therapy, would think he was a psychiatric assistant or a student in some area of health. But today Jonas
couldn't linger. Letícia was alone in the house. If something unexpected came up, she could get scared and take
off, ruining everything.

At noon, Jonas saw Dr. Nesse leave the main building
and head to the cafeteria. He noticed that the doctor
paused when he saw him and then continued on his
path. Jonas didn't wait for him to finish his lunch. He
headed back to Ipanema, locked up his bike, and bought
food for another day.

Letícia had showered again and was drying her hair
beside the window when she saw Jonas opening the gate.
He made his way slowly, carrying a bag of groceries in
each hand. It was almost two when he entered the bedroom, visibly tired.

"What took you so long? I was afraid, all alone here."

"I told you this place is perfectly safe. The pastor only
comes on weekends and nobody else has the key."

"But all you had to do was stick your hand inside the
light fixture."

"I'd arranged it with him. And besides, the people in
the favela don't bother the people on the street. It's an
unwritten rule, but it's the law."

"Fine, but I want you to stay here with me."

"We've got the rest of the afternoon and all night to be together. Isn't that what you told your mom? Two days at your friend's house?"

"Right. I just hope she isn't going around calling all my friends to make sure."

"Do you want to leave?"

"No. I just want to enjoy the time we still have left."

While he was taking his purchases out of the bags and arranging them on top of the dresser, Jonas watched Letícia brushing her hair, sitting on the bed, wrapped in a towel.

"I saw your father today."

"What do you mean?"

"I went to the hospital."

"You left me here alone and went to the hospital? What were you doing there?"

"I just needed to see how your father was doing."

"Why did you need to do that?"

"To see if he was okay."

"I don't get it. We spent so much time talking about how we could spend a couple of days together, just the two of us, in a pleasant place, where nobody could find us. You get this great house for free. I make up a story, which I'm not sure my mother believed, we come here, spend a wonderful night, and the next day you leave me here by myself to go check up on my dad? Is that right, or did I miss something?"

"That's right. What I don't know is if you and I see it the same way. I didn't leave you alone *in order to check up on your dad.* I went to get some food, since we didn't have anything else to eat. I needed to see how your dad was doing, not because I was worried about his health, but because I was worried about yours. I wanted to see if he'd figured out that you weren't with a girlfriend. That's why I let him see me. Depending on his reaction, I'd know how things stood. When he reacted normally, I decided everything was fine. I bought some things and came back. As you can see, the facts are the same, but the meaning is different."

"Then take off your clothes and come to bed."

It was the second night Letícia had spent away from home. Dr. Nesse had already convinced himself that his daughter hadn't been kidnapped but that, in cahoots with Jonas, she had run away. The note the boy had delivered didn't reveal anything; it just made clear who, at that time, was in command of the situation. The doctor hadn't said anything to his wife or other daughter, but they all knew that Letícia had disappeared and that they had to do everything possible to bring her back home. Everyone was trying to understand what had happened, but they weren't privy to all the information Dr. Nesse had. Their guesses, including the maid's, were products of their own imaginations.

Thursday night was sleepless for everyone. When they sat down for breakfast the next day, Dr. Nesse was still hoping that Roberta, the younger daughter, might reveal some secret, big or small, that would help move the investigation along; or that the maid would remember some snippet of conversation between Letícia and a girlfriend; or even that his wife would recall some information her daughter had confided.

The policeman had said that if there was no news they would start looking in twenty-four hours. Even if he didn't believe she'd been kidnapped, Dr. Nesse would have to cooperate with the investigation. There was still the possibility, which nobody dared say out loud but which threatened to crash through the silence at any moment, that Letícia was dead. Reminding the three women of this, Dr. Nesse had stressed that any information, any clue, no matter how insignificant, could be greatly useful in locating Letícia.

At nine in the morning, they heard the sound of a key in the lock. The door sprang open. Letícia gave the group a terrified look before entering.

After the moment of shock had passed, her mother jumped out of her seat to hug her.

"What happened, sweetie? You weren't with your friends. . . . Two days . . ."

"I needed to find out if he was crazy."

"Where were you?" her father asked.

"I was with Jonas . . . I didn't believe that he was crazy. . . . Now I'm sure he's not."

"I didn't ask if he was crazy, because I already know he is; I asked where you were."

"In a house, up on the Rua Saint Roman. A kind of church."

"A church?"

"I'm not sure—I didn't see anything, nobody was there."

"Jonas took you there?"

"That's right."

"And what did he do?"

"He was with me the whole time."

"He couldn't have been there the whole time, since I saw him at the hospital at lunch yesterday."

"I know. He told me he was there. He wanted to see if you were okay."

"If I was okay! He locked you up in a house in the middle of a favela and came down to see how *I* was? And you say he's not crazy? He's crazy, and not a little crazy either."

"He's not, Dad."

"I'm a doctor! I'm his psychiatrist! I know what I'm talking about!"

"Dad, he's a great guy. He's not crazy."

"Teresa, talk to her, try to find out what happened. If it's necessary, take her to a doctor."

"I'm not going to a doctor! I'm not sick! You think everyone's sick! You're the sick one!"

Her father slapped her with such violence that Letícia fell against the door and collapsed to the floor.

"Nobody talks to me that way, and certainly not my

own daughter. You're an idiotic brat, underage besides, and yes, you are going to the doctor, even if I have to take you there by force."

—➤—

Dr. Nesse told Espinosa that his daughter had returned, and said that everything was all right with her.

"So your intervention is no longer necessary, sir. Besides, it happened just as you predicted. In any case, I thank you for your help."

"You don't want to file a complaint?"

"No, Officer. There's no reason; everything's under control. Thank you."

—➤—

On Monday, Dr. Nesse arrived at the hospital early.

"Good morning, Doctor."

"Morning. Any messages?"

"No, Doctor."

It was eight-thirty. He had some time before his first patient. With the blinds raised, he carefully examined the courtyard. He left the room and walked through the wing Jonas hung out in. He passed the cafeteria and the recreation room, went through the part of the courtyard he couldn't see from his office, and returned to his office just as his receptionist arrived. He told her to call him if Jonas was spotted in the hospital.

At five to nine, he was ready to see his first patient and Jonas still had not shown up. He didn't have an appointment today, but the doctor assumed that, as always, he would put in an appearance. At nine the first patient arrived. At nine-ten, Dr. Nesse looked through the window and spotted Jonas sitting on the bench under the mango tree, chatting with an inpatient. The doctor started to get up, but restrained himself. As soon as the appointment was over, he went out to the court-yard, but Jonas was no longer on the bench. He searched the parking lot, the entrance gate, and inside the hospi-tal, then went back to the entrance gate and interrogated the employee he'd seen talking with Jonas on other occa-sions, but there was no sign of him. Jonas had vanished.

Finishing up with his last patient of the morning, he couldn't remember a thing that had been said in the ses-sion. From a clinical perspective, the morning had been a disaster.

By the end of the afternoon, the headache he'd had since lunchtime had been joined by chills. In the car, he didn't turn on the air-conditioning, and at several points he was tempted to pull over. When he got home, he had a fever. He got in bed and slept.

He spent Tuesday in bed. Flu, his wife said.

It was hot on Wednesday, and the sky was blue. Dr. Nesse woke up ready to work. It was the day of Jonas's appointment, but Dr. Nesse doubted that he'd dare show his face. He didn't want to be surprised as he'd been Monday, seeing him disappear practically under his nose. Whatever story Jonas was going to come up with, he'd be ready for the counterattack.

Jonas wasn't at his usual spot at the entry gate. He wasn't in the parking lot or under the mango tree. When Dr. Nesse returned to his office, after his coffee, however, he found Jonas in the treatment room, sitting in the patient's chair.

"What are you doing here?"

"Waiting for you, sir; it's time for my appointment."

"Why didn't you wait to be sent in by the receptionist?"

"She's the one who sent me in here, Doctor."

"What did you do with my daughter?"

"Nothing."

"You didn't do anything?"

"No. At least nothing wrong."

"And what you did to her in that house on the Rua Saint Roman, that wasn't anything? Do you realize that you disappeared for two days with a minor?"

"I didn't disappear. I was even here in the hospital—you saw me yourself. I didn't know that Letícia was a minor. I never asked her how old she was, and she never asked me. She doesn't look underage."

"Why did you give us a false address?" Dr. Nesse placed Jonas's chart on top of the table.

"I didn't give a false address—they might have written it down wrong." Jonas picked up the paper, looked at it, and gave it back to the doctor. "The address is right. I live in an old building and the entrance is a door between two shops. You might not have seen it. You can go check it out yourself."

"Come back tomorrow, at the same time."

"What about our appointment?"

"Come back tomorrow."

Jonas got up from the chair and waited for the doctor to say something. He didn't look indignant, angry, or scared. He looked as serene as always. He left, wishing the doctor a nice day.

Dr. Nesse had resisted mentioning the note. If Jonas's intention had been to alarm him, he'd never know what effect the note had had on him. Sooner or later he'd be reduced to asking the receptionist if the note had been delivered. It would be his confession of guilt.

He sent for the next patient. Only with great effort did he manage to conduct the session. Letícia's phrases about Jonas and the house on the Rua Saint Roman kept coming to mind, mixing in with the words of his patient, a twenty-year-old girl. Sometimes he even mixed up their faces. The same happened with his afternoon patients in his private practice.

He didn't have the nerve to tell his wife—she wouldn't understand. And he thought it best not to discuss the matter with a colleague: such things were hard to take back once they'd been said, and could even leak out and damage his professional reputation. He couldn't tell anyone how much the case was getting to him. He had to keep it to himself and try to deal with it all bit by bit, on his own. Just like crazy people did.

It was after eleven o'clock when, already stretched out in bed, he took off his pajamas and got dressed to go out. He gathered his wallet and key chain and left the house without bothering to answer his wife when she asked what was going on. He retrieved the car from the garage and made his way down the street, heading nowhere in particular. He didn't feel like listening to music. He wandered around for about half an hour. On the Avenida Atlântica, he had to slow down to weave his way through the prostitutes and transsexuals on the curb. A single man in a fancy car at that hour guaranteed an exhibition of breasts and butts. Dr. Nesse kept the windows up and the doors locked. He cruised along the beach in both directions and went back to Ipanema. He headed toward the Praça General Osório and ended up on the Rua Jangadeiros. He stopped in front of the number Jonas had given. There was, in fact, a door wedged between two storefronts. At that hour, the stores were closed; the only light to be seen was behind the cast-iron gate. There was no doorman in sight.

The existence of the building confirmed what the guy had said, but it didn't guarantee that he actually lived there. The street was quiet at night. He double-parked in front of the building, turning off the motor and his lights, and waited. After a while, the heat became unbearable. He opened the front windows. The heat diminished, but he was nervous. Clearly he wasn't cut out to be a spy.

It was almost two in the morning when he woke the night guard at the hospital. He drove into the lot, parked, cracked the windows, leaned back, and slept until daybreak.

The city was beginning its morning movement: cafés, bakeries, and newspaper vendors were greeting their first clients when Dr. Nesse crossed the street that separated the university campus from the café to get some breakfast. On the way back, he bought a razor at a newspaper kiosk, then shaved in the doctors' bathroom and waited for the first employees to arrive.

He had all his morning appointments canceled, with the exception of Jonas's. He gave a few instructions to his receptionist, locked himself in his office, and waited. The emptiness and discomfort of the room set his mind wandering, since there was nothing in there that could claim his attention, and he had almost two hours before the guy arrived. His body ached from the night he'd spent in the car. His face and hands were covered with mosquito bites. As he waited, Dr. Nesse made several notes on the patient's chart and gave a few instructions to the nursing staff over the interphone.

At ten o'clock the receptionist announced Jonas and sent him in. Dr. Nesse sat looking at his patient for a while. Jonas asked if they were going to have a regular session. Instead of answering, the doctor picked up the interphone, mumbled a few words, leapt out of his chair, pushed a few objects from his desk onto the floor, and grabbed Jonas from behind in a stranglehold. The kid thrashed about as the doctor held him by the neck. In a few seconds two nurses entered the room with orders to

sedate the patient, who had suffered a psychotic out-
break during his treatment. Jonas was contained and
medicated.

The employees felt sorry for the guy, whom they all
considered so intelligent and polite, but they agreed that
that was how it was: the quieter the patient, the more
furious the storm.

On the first day, Dr. Nesse kept Jonas strongly sedated.
On the two following days, he cut back on the medication, enough to keep him awake.

On the afternoon of the fourth day, Sunday, Jonas
could be seen seated on the stone bench beneath the
mango tree. He didn't speak to anyone or respond to the
voices directed at him. On Monday morning, Dr. Nesse
tried to get in touch with his parents, but nobody
answered at the telephone number Jonas had provided.
Up until then, only the medical team knew about his
internment.

Letícia found out almost two weeks later. The episode
in the Rua Saint Roman had led to a state of practical
incarceration: she could leave to go to school, but nothing else. If she wanted to study with friends, they had to
come to her house. Entertainment and excursions in the
neighborhood were forbidden by her father. She hadn't
spoken to Jonas since they had disappeared together.

There was no answer at Jonas's number, which she

found in her father's appointment book. She remembered that he went to the hospital on Wednesdays. She called the hospital on Tuesday morning, claiming to be Dr. Nesse's secretary, to confirm the next day's appointments. When the operator gave a list of patients that didn't include Jonas, Letícia asked if the name Jonas appeared anywhere, as it was in the doctor's schedule. The woman answered that Jonas had been hospitalized and that his weekly sessions had been suspended.

It was after one in the afternoon when Letícia introduced herself at the reception area as Dr. Nesse's daughter.

"Your father already left, about fifteen minutes ago."

"Thanks, but I didn't come for him, I came to see an acquaintance who's been hospitalized."

"Is he in the infirmary?"

"I don't know."

"What's his name?"

"Jonas."

"He's a good kid. He spent the morning on the stone bench. If you turn right, heading toward the courtyard, you'll see a big mango tree. There's a stone bench underneath, and that's where he usually is."

From a distance, Letícia recognized the figure under the tree. She came up slowly, without waving or calling his name. She almost touched him before he noticed her. His eyes were glazed over, and his body was limp. She sat down beside him.

"Hi, Jonas."

He didn't answer, move, or even look at her; he kept staring at the thick root of the tree his foot was resting upon.

"I understand that you don't want to talk to me, but I had nothing to do with what happened. I only found out that you were here yesterday afternoon."

Jonas didn't seem to register anything she was saying.

"Is there anything I can do to get you out of here?"

"I don't want to get out of here," he said in a rough, husky voice.

"You don't want to leave?"

"No."

"Jonas, this isn't the place for you."

"Why not?"

"Because you're not crazy!"

"Now I am."

"No you're not! You can't go crazy just because my dad wants you to be. Have you forgotten about the two days we spent together?"

He kept staring at the tree's roots, as if they contained all the answers to her questions.

Letícia's eyes filled with tears and she put her arm around his shoulders. During the long silence, she hugged him without receiving a word, look, or gesture in response. She decided simply to talk to him, without expecting acknowledgment. She told him what she thought of the whole thing; she talked about her father; she talked about their two days in the house on the Rua Saint Roman; she talked about what she planned to do from that day forward. She talked for almost two hours, and then got up and left.

That night, during dinner, she informed her father of her decision to enter the hospital with Jonas, adding that if he tried to stop her she would do something that would necessarily lead to her being taken to a psychiatric emergency room. It would be better, therefore, for him to agree to have her sent to the same hospital where he worked, because that way she could keep a close eye on Jonas's treatment. The next morning, when he arrived at the hospital, she would already be waiting for him.

Dr. Nesse heard out her threats in silence. He had promised his wife that he would control his reactions, especially any new impulse to hit his daughter. That moment his promise was put to the test for the first time. Of course, he wouldn't agree to committing her to a psychiatric hospital just so she could keep her boyfriend company. Letícia had never been much given to flights of that kind; she'd always been a calm, obedient girl. He didn't answer his daughter's declarations.

The next morning, when he arrived at the hospital, he was informed that a girl was there claiming to be his daughter and asking to be admitted. Without offering explanations to anyone, Dr. Nesse put his daughter in the car, by force, took her home, and left her locked in her room, under her mother's eye. He went back to the hospital to complete his morning rounds.

Just before lunchtime, his secretary interrupted his last appointment to inform him that the chief of the emergency ward at the Hospital Pinel needed to speak to him urgently. Letícia had been taken there, picked up by a police patrol, after being seen walking stark naked down the Avenida Atlântica, in front of the Copacabana Palace. A hotel employee had given her a pool towel for her to cover herself before the police car arrived.

A few minutes later, a nurse, accompanied by the police officers who had answered the call, brought Letícia to her father's office, still wrapped in the hotel towel. She was left with Dr. Nesse after he signed a paper taking responsibility for her.

As soon as they were alone, Letícia announced that if her father tried to remove her from the building her next act would make the episode on the Avenida Atlântica seem like a joke. Dr. Nesse decided not to take chances and kept her sedated and under his care in the hospital for the rest of the day. There was no way to try to preserve his professional image in front of his colleagues and employees: the damage was done. He managed to sequester his daughter in a small room designed for emergency treatment, and arranged for two nurses to keep an eye on her. He considered the possibility of transferring her the next day to a private clinic.

The next morning, dressed in clothes her mother had brought the night before, and still a little drowsy from the medication, Letícia sought out Jonas in the courtyard. She found him on the bench, from which he seemingly hadn't budged. She sat beside him.

"Now we're together, Jonas."

He didn't reply or even look at her. Letícia put her hand on his.

"Did you hear me, Jonas? Now I'm with you."

No reaction. Jonas kept his gaze on the roots beneath the bench.

"It's fine. I don't feel like talking either. Maybe later."

⯈

That same day, after his morning appointments, Dr. Nesse informed his daughter that he would release Jonas in a day or two. He also broke the news to Jonas personally, and prescribed a new medication.

"Just another day or two, and you'll be free to go home. You'll only need to come to the hospital for checkups and to pick up your medicine."

"I'm fine here."

"I know you're fine; that's why I'm releasing you."

"I'm not done with what I came to do."

"We can continue the treatment. Your appointment will remain the same."

Jonas didn't answer or move from his spot on the bench. Dr. Nesse thought it was a matter of time. His daughter would return to normal as well, as soon as Jonas was out of the hospital.

⯈

Dr. Nesse had his daughter transferred to the same clinic where he sent his private patients. He didn't intend to keep her there longer than strictly necessary;

he saw her crisis as nothing more than a phase. It didn't meet any usual description of psychosis, and she wasn't delirious or hallucinating. Letícia was intellectually intact. Only one detail gave Dr. Nesse pause: from the moment he'd transferred her from the hospital to the clinic, Letícia had stopped speaking to him. She didn't address him or answer his questions. On the day she left the clinic, her mother picked her up, as she refused to go home with her father.

Letícia never again asked about Jonas. Sometimes she spent full days without speaking to anyone, and when she did it was only to reply in monosyllables to some question posed by her mother or sister. After a while, she stopped speaking entirely.

In spite of his release, Jonas hadn't left the hospital. But he didn't resist when they placed his things in a bag and took him to the gate, leaving him outside. The employee congratulated him and wished him luck.

"Thank you, but I can't leave yet."

"You can come back whenever you want, Jonas."

"I still can't leave."

"We like you, Jonas, but you're better off at home, with your family. Would you rather stay here in the hospital eating this shitty food and sleeping with all these smelly inpatients?"

Jonas stood there, bag in hand, and stared at the courtyard.

"Jonas, this isn't the place for a guy like you. Go home, buddy."

"I'd rather stay."

He went back through the gate and walked slowly toward the courtyard. He spent the rest of the afternoon seated on his stone bench with his bag clutched to his body on the ground beside him. And from that day forth he left the stone bench only to use the bathroom or, at night, to find a place to sleep in the infirmary. During the day, even when it was raining, he sat under the mango tree. He politely refused all offers of assistance. More than once people tried to remove him, but he returned patiently to the bench. He was never hostile or aggressive toward the staff. After every removal he thanked them kindly and retraced his steps after a few minutes.

Letícia no longer showed up to chat, and days later he learned that while he had been interned she had been transferred to a private clinic. He stopped appearing in the cafeteria at mealtimes and only reluctantly accepted the bowls of soup brought to him by the staff. As the days went by, people began to find him on the bench, no longer sitting but stretched out on it, using his bag as a pillow. He grew thinner every day. His former grace was now fragility. After he'd spent two days straight on the bench, they took him to the infirmary and began feeding him intravenously. Despite his extreme weakness, he was to be seen the next morning on his bench. They carried him back to the infirmary. When Dr. Nesse was called to make a decision about what to do next, he found Jonas tied to the bedposts, his eyes wide open.

"Why are you doing this?"

"This what, Doctor?"

"This scene."

"Scene? Like the one you set up in your office? And then the order to lock up your daughter? Are you going to commit the whole family?"

"Who are you?"

"Jonas. Isidoro. The name doesn't matter."

"What are you planning to do?"

"I still haven't decided."

"Why are you doing this?"

The young man closed his eyes, visibly tired by the effort, undermined by the medication, thin, poorly fed. Dr. Nesse stood beside the bed, waiting for a response that never came.

The next day, on Dr. Nesse's orders, Jonas was transferred to a general hospital. His physical state demanded immediate care. It was a routine decision, since the psychiatric hospital didn't have an intensive therapy unit or resources for the kind of treatment he required. Before patients deteriorated to a critical point, they were always removed to a general public hospital.

The patients Jonas had befriended looked for him on the bench over the next few days. Two weeks after his disappearance, they stopped asking about him. It didn't take long for them to forget their friend. Jonas was remembered only two months later, when the news arrived at the hospital that he had disappeared.

STORY NUMBER TWO

After almost seven months, Espinosa didn't remember if he'd kept the card the doctor had given him, but he had a tin can, inherited from his grandmother, on the shelf in the living room, where he kept every kind of card—from friends, from the guy who fixed the refrigerator, from the garage, from pharmacies, pizzerias, restaurants. . . . It didn't take him long to find Dr. Artur Nesse's. Since it was eight-thirty at night, he assumed the doctor would be home. The person who answered the phone sounded like a recorded message as she recited the information: "Dr. Nesse no longer lives here. Please try his office. The number may be found . . ." He didn't ask if the whole family had moved or if Dr. Nesse alone had left home. He called the office, and the answering machine picked up. There was little difference between it and the person he'd just spoken to. He wouldn't try anywhere else that night.

He called the psychiatrist's office again the following afternoon, when he actually spoke to a flesh-and-blood human, who connected him with the doctor.

"Dr. Nesse, I don't know if you still remember me. It's Chief Espinosa."

"Of course, of course, sir. And how are you?"

"Fine, thanks."

"Is there a problem, Officer?"

"We need to talk, Doctor."

"My daughter . . . ?"

"No, Doctor, it's concerning you."

"Did something else happen?"

"Something *else*?"

"Sorry, Officer, but stuff's been happening lately."

"Why don't we meet at that same bench in the square in the Peixoto District?"

"Fine . . . but is it something serious?"

"I still don't know; it might be nothing. How's eight-thirty tonight?"

"Fine. Eight-thirty . . . same bench . . . Peixoto."

"Okay, I'll see you then, Doctor."

It was five-thirty in the afternoon, not a lot was going on at the station, and Espinosa let himself leave a little earlier than usual to go check out the secondhand-book store that had opened a few months before, only a block away. The owner had just received a nice lot of books from a widow whose husband, it was said, had good taste in literature. Espinosa wanted to be among the first to sift through it. Happily for his cleaning lady, the means at Espinosa's disposal for purchasing books were limited. Even so, it was an unusual month in which his library was not enriched by at least a half dozen acquisitions. This would not have been a problem for the maid if he had owned any shelving, which would have facilitated her cleaning work enormously. All there was, however, was a singular piece of domestic engineering occupying the entirety of the longest wall in the living room. It was a shelfless shelving system: the shelves were made up of books, which allowed him to dispense with the use of wood or any other material. A library in its purest state: first, a row of upright books; then, atop those, books laid horizontally; then another row of upright books; and so on. The contraption was already taller than Espinosa, and the maid opined that its balance was ever more precarious.

So at the end of that winter day, Espinosa was hoping to contribute a few more pieces to the still-distant but increasingly inexorable moment when his shelfless shelving system would collapse. The trip from the station to his house didn't necessarily require a swing by the bookstore. He could choose between two direct routes and one more-or-less direct route: the first and most direct, down the Rua Tonelero, had nothing further to recommend it; the second, down the Rua Barata Ribeiro, included, only steps from the station, the bookstore; and the third, the least direct, included a passage through the Galeria Menescal, where there was no bookstore but there was the Arab guy selling kibbeh. He took the last route when he needed something extra for dinner; the meat altered the monotonous menu of frozen spaghetti and lasagna. That night, Espinosa opted for pasta and books. The meatballs could wait.

It was June; the night was cold, and most of the trees were bare. This time the doctor arrived in a taxi, rather than in his fancy foreign car. He seemed to have been wearing the same suit for weeks: the shirt was rumpled and the tie barely loosened from his neck. He didn't immediately recognize the policeman.

"Dr. Nesse?"

"Chief Espinosa . . . sorry, I didn't see you."

"Shall we head for our bench?"

"Yes . . . of course. Let's go."

They crossed the street toward the square. Because of the time and the temperature, all the benches were free. Dr. Nesse's suit was of thin material, not appropriate for the weather, but he didn't seem to notice. Espinosa was wearing an overcoat that kept him perfectly warm.

"Sorry about the inconvenience of the meeting, Doctor, but just like last time I didn't want to do anything on the record."

"What's the matter, Officer?" The doctor's voice was lower than usual.

Espinosa took a folded piece of paper out of his coat, opened it, and handed it to the doctor.

"I got this letter a few days ago from the chief of the Tenth Precinct, who remembered the episode with your daughter and someone who, at the time, had made a reference to me. The letter came to him via a staff member at the hospital where you work, a person who asked not to be identified. It seems an identical letter was sent to the Board of Medicine."

Dr. Nesse put on his reading glasses and found a place where the paper would be illuminated by the lamps in the square. The text was computer-generated and had been printed out single-spaced, in a small font covering the whole page. The style was simple, direct, unadorned. The doctor read and reread the letter. After he was done, he handed it back to Espinosa.

"You didn't need to call me about this. It's the typical product of a paranoiac."

"In the letter you're being accused of homicide . . ."

"Premeditated homicide. Do you believe the letter of a crazy person?"

"I'm not a doctor, Dr. Nesse, I'm a policeman."

"That letter would never stand up in court."

"It's a well-written, logically consistent letter. The description of how you faked the guy's attack in order to keep him interned and under medication is rather objective, even providing the names of the nurses you called to subjugate him. . . . It doesn't strike me as a crazy person's letter."

"But it is."

"The hospital staff all describe the guy as a polite, friendly person who was never aggressive toward anyone. Even if you thought he was crazy, there's no record of any physical violence that he committed against anyone. And what this letter asserts is that the only person who used violence was you yourself, and that the violence you used killed the patient."

"That's insane."

"Maybe."

"You can't be serious, Chief."

"Let's just go over some of the facts, Doctor. First, you come to the police to say that your daughter had been kidnapped. Then, you say that you know the kidnapper's name but won't reveal it, citing professional ethics. The next day, you report that your daughter has come home safe and sound. A few days later, a police car picks up your daughter walking down the Avenida Atlântica naked, and you place her in the same hospital where you work. Two weeks earlier, you commit a patient, the alleged kidnapper of your daughter. That patient is transferred from your hospital and eventually dies after a series of other transfers. But before he dies, he writes this letter and gives it to a hospital staff member, recommending that it be given to the police in the event of his death. What do you think about that?"

"I think you're being taken in by the ravings of someone who is completely delirious. There are extremely elaborate deliriums, Officer. A delirious discourse is a fiction the patient uses to exorcise the world that threatens him. In itself, the fiction can seem perfectly logical, except for the simple fact that it has no relationship to reality. As for sending a copy to the Board of Medicine, I'm not worried about that. The doctors on the board are perfectly capable of distinguishing delirium from reality."

"I don't look at things from a medical point of view, Doctor. I received a written denunciation, signed by a patient of yours, claiming to be a victim of medical abuses and in fear of his life. That person disappeared shortly thereafter, in murky circumstances. None of that is delirium, Dr. Nesse."

"He was transferred from the hospital because he was on a hunger strike and was in terrible physical condition. A psychiatric hospital is not a general hospital. He needed specialized treatment. The transfer was made in order to save his life. Did he die or disappear? What does the autopsy say?"

"There's no autopsy."

"What do you mean? He didn't die in a hospital?"

"We don't know."

"What about his parents?"

"We couldn't find his parents."

"And what about him? Where did they find him?"

"He hasn't been found."

"So how do you know he's dead?"

"We don't."

"There was no burial?"

"Nobody knows. One idea is that he was buried in a pauper's grave, but for that to happen the body would be registered at the Forensic Institute. We checked out all the cases over the last few months. None matches."

"And what do they say at the hospital?"

"The last entry in his chart is a request for a transfer, but there's no record of his having left. He disappeared inside the hospital when he could barely stand up."

"And what do I have to do with that disappearance?"

"I hope nothing—"

"So—"

"Except the letter and the fact that only a doctor can authorize a patient's release, even a temporary release."

When nothing interrupted the silence following Espinosa's statement, Dr. Nesse saw a taxi letting out a passenger, mumbled some words of farewell, and left.

Espinosa remained seated on the bench for a few more minutes. The cool air was not unpleasant and helped clear his head. The doctor had reacted to the letter with indifference, even before he knew there was no proof that the guy was dead. Unless he knew what had been done with the body.... But if the letter didn't affect him, something else, something major, had already hit him. His careless dress, his rumpled appearance, his indifference to the news, his lack of interest in his future: none of this fit the man he'd met a few months ago. Something much more important than the letter had affected him.

Espinosa got up from the bench and started walking around the square—the same distance as a lap around a block—before heading back to his apartment. He still couldn't decide whether he thought better seated or standing. Most of the time, he just let his ideas flow. His mind waged a continual struggle between reason and imagination, with the latter clearly predominating. His involvement with the letter was yet another proof. There was no case. The only thing they had was a letter of dubious attribution. The content may have been authentic—the witnesses seemed to confirm it—but there was no guarantee that it had been written by Jonas, or Isidoro, if those were even real names. Besides, no formal or even verbal complaint regarding his mistreatment had been lodged. As for the supposed murder, it might not be anything more than a fantasy on the part of the staff member who'd turned over the letter. Fantasy, or bad faith. The letter was not handwritten, which made it seem less authentic. There was a signature— rather, there were two signatures, Jonas's, and then, in parentheses, Isidoro's. Neither included a surname. But above all, there was no body, and without a body there was no crime. The best thing for him to do, then, was to keep the letter, get the wine out of the refrigerator—a souvenir from his last encounter with Irene—stick something in the microwave, and enjoy the evening with one of the books he'd bought that evening.

While he awaited the three beeps from the microwave that signaled the arrival of his lasagna, Espinosa thought about a certain kind of person who buzzed around other people's lives like a fly, unsure whether to stay or go, flitting all around but always returning to the same point. That was how he thought of Dr. Nesse: an immense, uncomfortable blowfly.

Ever since the station had been remodeled, Espinosa had lost his daily bearings. It wasn't just that the look had changed, the old, dusty building transformed into something more high-tech, the new computers replacing mountains of files, cases, memos, and records. Every once in a while he found himself missing the tapping of typewriters, which had been replaced by the almost inaudible sound of computer keyboards. With so much less stuff around, there were also fewer people around to deal with it. But the most notable change had been the elimination of the holding cells. The only cell in the new station was a little room containing a cot, a sink, and a toilet, which could hold only one prisoner. The station had been streamlined, but the old mentality of most of the inhabitants remained. Not everyone, though. There were a few cops who still hadn't been tainted by corruption. One of them was Welber.

"Chief, have you decided if we're going to take care of the doctor's case?"

"It's not ours, it's the Tenth Precinct's."

"But they sent it over to us. Not officially, of course."

"No, because officially there's no case. Murder? Where's the body? Is there any material proof that anybody's died? We don't have anything, Welber. The only thing we've got is a computer-printed letter with a name—actually, two names—that isn't even a signature."

"So it's ours?"

"Why?"

"You said 'the only thing we've got.' That means you're already thinking of it as our case, even if we don't have anything yet."

"Fine. Let's register it and check out where all the information has come from. You've got two weeks to find out everything you can on the guy. Go back to the hospital where he was and see if you can get any names of the staff on duty the day he disappeared or was released; check around to see if anyone saw a doctor who looked like Dr. Nesse; afterward go to the Tenth and see if you can determine who gave the letter to the doctor. Get their complete name, address, and phone number. If that turns up any information about the guy's death, then we have a case; if not, send the letter back to the Tenth for their files and drop the whole matter."

Welber had begun his career on Espinosa's team of detectives, when he was an inspector in the downtown precinct, in the Praça Mauá. Back then, he was barely twenty years old, a fresh recruit from the police academy who didn't think that being a cop and being honest were mutually exclusive; and Espinosa gave him the chance to prove it. They'd worked together ever since, with a brief hiatus when Welber was recovering from a bullet wound that had cost him his spleen and almost cost him his life. The bullet had been meant for Espinosa. Ever since that incident, they'd been friends. When Espinosa was named chief of the Twelfth Precinct, his first action was to make sure Welber got transferred to the same station.

Irene didn't like calling the station; she always thought she was interfering with some important investigation—and Espinosa wasn't about to knock down the good image she had of the police and of his work as a policeman. What she couldn't imagine was that more often than not he was fighting not bandits but his own incapacity for certain complex operations on the computer: in this case, the complex operation involved searching for something on the Internet. It was six-thirty in the evening.

"Hey, hon, how 'bout dinner?"

"Great. I'll come pick you up at eight-thirty."

"Perfect. Till then."

The two of them had a few things in common, and one of them was an aversion to the telephone. They kept their conversation to what was strictly necessary, a rule they broke only when they were in different cities and hadn't seen each other for a long time.

Irene was a lot younger than Espinosa and had entered his life just as he was completing a decade of bachelorhood, on the heels of a decade of marriage that had ended in divorce. But she nurtured no desire to become the second Mrs. Espinosa. "Every time I hear the word 'marriage,' I always think of a corset: either because it's so old-fashioned or because it's so suffocating," she'd once said. Irene had nothing against marriage in general; it was just how she felt about marriage for herself, which didn't bother Espinosa. They'd had only one conversation on the subject, treating the topic as a thesis

to attack or defend, but not as something that had anything to do with them personally. The question had
already been decided. At least, that's what they each
gave the other to understand.

~

Seeing Espinosa seated in front of her in the restaurant, Irene wondered what it was about him that made
him attractive. He wasn't particularly handsome and
he didn't have any special physical characteristics. Yet
it was impossible not to notice him, even when he did
his best to pass unnoticed. The way he walked, talked,
looked, and listened made him an absolutely singular
person, and this would have been the case whether he'd
been an engineer, pharmacist, or painter. But what she
was most fascinated by was the bizarre combination of
logical thinking and delirious fantasy that cohabited in
his head.

"What are you thinking about?" he asked.

"You."

"And?"

"And I've decided you're an almost impossible being."

"Nice, the 'almost.'"

"What's bothering you?"

"You think something's bothering me?"

"Isn't it?"

"Maybe."

"And what is it?"

"Almost everything . . . or almost nothing."

"You always try to wiggle through with answers like that."

"But I'm being sincere."

"Maybe in relation to my question, but it's not sincere in relation to yourself."

"Irene, when you ask me if something's bothering me and I say yes, almost everything or almost nothing, that means that what's bothering me isn't quite a worry. Being concerned about a person, a situation, a specific danger—that's part of my daily life. It's uncomfortable, but it doesn't really get under my skin. What's bothering me is completely different: it's not a thing, it's not a person, it's not a situation, it's nothing in particular, but it's very strong, and it pains me through and through . . ."

"Espinosa, when was the last time we had sex?"

⟶

For two days, Welber interrogated doctors, nurses, and staff members from the last hospital where Jonas had stayed before his disappearance. After more than three months, nobody remembered much of anything. Because so many patients came and went in the big public hospital, it was almost impossible for anyone to remember a specific patient after so much time. Some vaguely remembered a young, tall, and very thin patient, but nothing more. The signature on the paperwork was just a stamp, and there was no note of the hospital where he'd been taken for tests. Even the reason for his departure was vague: additional testing. Asked about a tall, plump doctor with very white skin who might have accompanied the patient on his departure, nobody could recall a thing. There was still the possibility that Jonas had left the hospital of his own free will, assuming he was able to walk. The paperwork authorizing his departure could have been completed by Jonas himself. In such an enormous hospital, anyone who wasn't dressed like a patient could walk around without being bothered.

On the afternoon of the third day, Welber figured it would be useless to continue hounding the hospital staff and decided to track down the woman Jonas had given the letter to. Then he would talk to Dr. Nesse, his wife, and his daughters. He had ten days to see where the information had come from.

The Tenth Precinct is two subway stops away from the Twelfth, in Copacabana. Welber called ahead to see if Chief Ferreira was around before leaving his home station on a pretty winter morning. He wanted to talk to Ferreira before he left for lunch.

The Botafogo station occupied an old colonial house, redesigned to accommodate a police station, not far from the subway station. The neighborhood still preserved a few mansions from the era when it was home to the aristocracy of Rio de Janeiro. The police station was not one of those mansions, but it must have been a pleasant upper-middle-class house. Chief Ferreira hadn't gone out for lunch and was waiting for him in his office.

"Excuse me, sir, I'm Detective Welber from the Twelfth Precinct. I called half an hour ago."

"Come in, Welber. Is it about the letter?"

"Yes, sir. I'm supposed to perform a preliminary investigation, and I wanted to know if you have any information about the person who delivered the letter."

"Not really. I wasn't here when she arrived. The letter was delivered sealed, addressed to me, and the woman who delivered it said it was extremely important. The detective on duty took down her name, address, and phone number. She said that she still worked at the same hospital. When I opened the letter, I didn't immediately make the connection, until I remembered the case of the daughter of the doctor at the psychiatric hospital who'd been taken to the Hospital Pinel by a police patrol."

"Did you ever speak to the woman? The one who brought the letter?"

"No, never."

"Could you give me her information?"

"All I have is her name, address, and phone number."

"That's fine, sir . . . if they're real."

Before he left the station, Welber tried the number the detective had taken down. He got an answering machine. The address was in Méier. It was pretty far for him to chance a surprise visit. But the hospital was only a fifteen-minute trip. He could walk to the university campus and eat lunch in the cafeteria there after speaking with the staff member.

Solange was the employee responsible for scheduling outpatients and sending them to the office of the doctor treating them. She'd seen Jonas every time he came in to see Dr. Nesse. Looking at her, Welber tried to imagine how far the friendship had gone between receptionist and patient. Solange was fair-skinned, with light eyes and hair, and was over thirty-five. She didn't seem impressed when Welber identified himself. She looked him straight in the eyes; her voice was pleasant.

"How did your friendship begin?"

"I think it was the first time I met him."

"What happened?"

"It's hard to say. Nothing really—he was just looking at me for a few seconds and I saw that there was a sweetness in his eyes. I have to say I was captivated by those eyes: he seemed to be looking for something he'd lost. Only much later did I understand that it was a cry for help."

"Why do you think that? Had something happened?"

"No. It was the first time I'd seen him."

"Did he talk to you? Did he tell you why he was coming for treatment?"

"He was very shy . . . or reserved. . . . He looked a lot, and he had a soft voice, like a poet's."

"He didn't talk about himself? About why he'd come here?"

"No. He never talked about himself or his family. He seemed more interested in Dr. Nesse. But that's how it is: those patients always want to know about the doctors' private lives."

"And when did you become more intimate?"

"Detective, you misunderstand me. We were never intimate. We never dated, if that's what you want to know. We just chatted a few times. He was a very nice person—you should have seen how he talked to the inpatients. Everyone liked him. When he sat there under the mango tree, two or three of them would immediately show up to talk with him. He knew them all by name."

"If you weren't so close, why do you think he left the letter with you?"

"I don't know. He was scared. I think he knew he could count on me."

"But that wasn't a first impression."

"Maybe it was. We always got on well. The situation with the letter came up much later, when Dr. Nesse's daughter showed up here. That's when Dr. Nesse started going crazy."

"Did he keep Jonas here because his daughter was interested in him?"

"The alleged motive was that Jonas had a crisis during the session, got violent, and had to be removed by force."

"Do you think that was the real reason?"

"Nobody who knew Jonas could imagine him attacking anyone, especially not the doctor. I don't know if the real reason was the girl, but it certainly wasn't that he'd attacked Dr. Nesse."

"And the girl?"

"The girl went completely crazy."

"What happened then?"

"Of course Dr. Nesse wouldn't let her stay here, like she wanted. He transferred her the next day to a private clinic. Then he arranged for Jonas to be transferred to a general hospital. That was when Jonas asked me to use the computer to write the letter."

"Was that allowed?"

"No. But it was only that one time. Besides, I thought he had plenty of reason to be scared."

"Why do you think that?"

"Because I do."

"Because you do? That's it?"

"Detective, this is a public hospital and I'm a public employee. My job could be endangered if it gets around that I'm giving out my opinion about the work of the doctors."

"You've helped a lot, Solange. Here's my card. If you remember anything else, please give me a call."

"Do you think that they'll get the guy?"

"What guy?"

"The guy who killed Jonas."

"Are you sure he's dead?"

"He isn't?"

"They still haven't found the body."

"Or found him alive."

"Thanks, Solange."

"No problem, Detective. Good luck."

Welber bid Solange farewell just as a short line was

starting to form in front of the cafeteria door. He didn't like the place. It was large and pretty, but the people were very strange. They looked like employees at a zoo, regarding the inpatients with the same standoffishness that zoo employees view animals. He had no desire to try the food at the hospital restaurant; he preferred to walk to the bus stop and head back to Copacabana. He reached the station just as Espinosa was leaving for lunch.

"Have you already eaten?" asked his boss.

"Not yet."

"Then let's go to the Italian place. You can fill me in."

The trattoria was three blocks from the station and was Espinosa's favorite spot for solitary lunches. Welber was one of the few he shared his table with. They went down the street in the direction of the Avenida Copacabana, where they turned left and walked toward the restaurant.

"What did you think of the girl?"

"I think she fell in love with Jonas during the time he was at the hospital. I couldn't figure out if the feeling was mutual, but it seems like the guy was nice and open enough to heighten her interest. She's a lot older than he is. It's not uninteresting. She's convinced that Jonas was killed. She thinks that Dr. Nesse was directly or indirectly responsible for his death, but she didn't have anything to back up that opinion. She says the letter is real, that it was typed on her computer and printed on her printer, while she was there."

"That proves who wrote the letter, but not necessarily the truth of its contents."

"But then why would he have written the letter?"

"Either because he was crazy or because he was really feeling threatened. That's the problem, Welber. When a crazy person says he's being persecuted, the persecutor can be either real or imaginary, but the feeling of being persecuted is real."

"According to Solange, the guy came to the hospital at the appointed times, talked to her after greeting the employees at the gate, and was sent in to see Dr. Nesse. Everyone, except the male nurses, said that Jonas was calm, peaceful, and didn't seem to have any physical tics. Less than two minutes later, the doctor had him in a headlock and the nurses ran into the room."

They were almost to the trattoria. The red Ferrari flag was displayed in the window, between the Brazilian and Italian flags, which meant that Ferrari had won the Formula One race the previous weekend.

They had an unspoken agreement never to talk about work over food. The agreement was usually respected. As they were sitting down, Welber ventured one more question.

"Did you ever meet Jonas?"

"No, I never saw him. I just know that he said his name was Jonas but his real name was Isidoro."

"He seemed to have a way with women."

"Why do you say that?"

"Because the woman I interviewed definitely had a

thing for him. The female staff members at the hospital sighed every time they mentioned him; and the doctor's daughter literally went crazy for him. I'm not trying to be funny, Chief, but that's how it was. The girl was perfectly normal and went insane, was sent to the hospital, and never recovered."

"People don't catch craziness like a cold."

"You don't think she was normal before?"

"I never met the girl, but I don't think that a normal adult goes crazy from one day to the next just because she met someone."

"Do you think Dr. Nesse is normal?"

"Why not? Because he was broken up by what happened to his daughter? Who wouldn't be?"

The next step was to talk to Dr. Nesse himself. The question was whether he would be willing to talk without being officially summoned. The detective was ready to hear a string of excuses before getting a clear refusal. But the doctor was very polite when he called. He had two openings in his schedule at the end of the afternoon and said that Welber was welcome to drop by his office.

It was ten to three. Welber had three hours before his meeting with the doctor. It was enough to digest his meal and to allow the effects of the wine he'd had with the risotto to disappear. There was still plenty of time to review the notes he'd made since the beginning of his investigation.

Everything seemed straightforward until Jonas was transferred from the psychiatric hospital. After that, the chain of events became vague, obscure. The shifts of the on-duty staff, along with the lack of precise records, made it almost impossible to follow all the steps of his treatment. Even the circumstances of Jonas's supposed death were shady. The most gaping lacuna was the staff's complete ignorance of what had happened to the body. He didn't think Dr. Nesse would be much help in clearing that up.

At the appointed hour, the detective rang the bell of the office and was greeted by the doctor himself. It wasn't a comfortable situation. Dr. Nesse was much older than he was, and was on his home terrain. And he hadn't been accused of anything. Yet there he was, a young detective, to ask questions about the doctor's hypothetical murder of a patient.

"Sorry, Officer, I didn't catch your name on the phone."

"Welber. Detective Welber from the Twelfth Precinct. Thanks for seeing me so soon, Doctor."

"More than anyone else, I want to see this misunderstanding cleared up once and for all. A lot of people have already suffered on account of it."

"If Jonas's death was confirmed, don't you think that things would go back to normal?"

"Some things never go back to normal, Detective. All we can do is be thankful that they still work, even defectively."

"Did you think Jonas was a hopeless case?"

"It depends on what you mean by hopeless. When

they're properly medicated, certain psychotics manage to maintain a degree of sociability. Isidoro—or Jonas—was indistinguishable from a normal person, except, of course, that he insisted his name was Jonas when his real name was Isidoro."

"When did you first notice that he was psychotic?"

"I started to realize how deeply disturbed Isidoro was—and I didn't know if it was psychotic or psychopathic—when he started coming to my house, following my daughter, even disappearing with her for two days, and when he started following me on his bike through the streets and interfering with my work at the hospital."

"Psychotic or psychopathic, you said . . ."

"Both can be equally aggressive and destructive."

"And that's what happened?"

"No question. At our last appointment he got up from his chair, grabbed a paperweight that was on the desk, and made a move as if to attack me. He only calmed down once he was sedated. After that, he was contained with medication. A layman would say he was calm. In fact he was sedated. If the medication were to be removed . . ."

"If he was under control, why did you transfer him to another hospital?"

"He stopped eating. He refused food. He became so physically weak that he had to be fed intravenously. I didn't think we had the proper facilities to treat him in the way he needed, so I ordered a transfer to a general hospital. I never saw him again."

"The letter says that you'd locked him up to keep him away from your daughter. And I've heard from staff members who believed that that was the reason you sent him to another hospital."

"I wouldn't give too much credence to that letter, Detective Welber. When Isidoro was transferred, my daughter had already suffered such a severe nervous collapse that she was being treated at a private clinic. There was no reason at all for me to send Isidoro anywhere."

"Given what happened between him and your daughter, didn't you think about killing him?"

"Absolutely."

"And what can you say to convince me you didn't?"

"It was no longer necessary. My daughter had already been affected. Killing him wouldn't be in self-defense; it would be revenge."

The conversation was briefer than Welber had expected. Shortly after six-thirty the detective left Ipanema and got on the first bus for Copacabana. At ten to seven he arrived at the station and went straight to Espinosa's office. He knew Espinosa would be waiting for him.

The boss had warned him that the doctor had a way with words, that he was a professional in the art of talking and listening, but Welber had left the office feeling that Dr. Nesse had been honest with him. He hadn't given any evasive answers or avoided responding to any of Welber's questions. His own admission that he had reason to kill Jonas was a courageous statement. Espinosa listened to Welber's story.

"Don't you think he was honest with me?"

"Maybe he doesn't even know himself."

"In any case, he didn't seem to have committed a crime, even though I heard a bit of guilt in his voice."

"He's got plenty of reasons to feel guilty, even if he hasn't committed a crime."

"There was only one thing that wasn't quite clear to me: Jonas's sudden transformation, in less than five minutes, from a normal person arriving for his weekly therapy session into a violent, dangerous psychopath who had to be forcefully restrained, medicated, and tied to a hospital bed."

"Maybe he's not the one who experienced the sudden transformation."

"You mean Dr. Nesse's the one who might have had a crisis?"

It was Friday. They left the station together. Espinosa only had a ten-minute walk; Welber could look forward to fifteen minutes on the subway to Tijuca, and then another stretch in the bus to his parents' house. He was saving for the down payment on an apartment. If he left home to live on his own, which was his fondest desire, he'd have to pay rent and he'd never be able to save up enough for a down payment. He wasn't thirty yet, but he was more than twenty-five, and every day he felt more and more restricted by his living arrangements.

On the sidewalk in front of the station, three cops

were discussing the capture of a drug dealer responsible for a large part of the traffic in Copacabana.

"One more who'll get an office in prison to keep on doing business on the outside," one of them said.

"Besides being conveniently close to his partners."

"What partners? The ones on their team or on ours?"

It was unclear how much of a joke that last line was. Welber felt the flow of his conversation with the chief had been broken. He also knew that Espinosa didn't like loose lips. And he suspected that what most bothered the boss was the suspicion that overhearing the three cops chatting outside the station, not far from where he was standing, was anything but accidental.

"Chief, we'll talk tomorrow."

"Fine. See you tomorrow, Welber."

It wasn't hard to get a seat on the subway at that hour. During the trip from Copacabana to Tijuca, Welber kept thinking about the conversation on the sidewalk and even wondered whether they'd overheard a fragment of a conversation or the whole conversation as they were intended to hear it. A message. In that club there were only two kinds of members: cops and dealers. Same club, same membership benefits for both.

Dr. Nesse stayed in his office for an hour after the detective left. He'd preferred to see the policeman as soon as possible. A delay could give rise to more detailed investigations and confused testimony from people who didn't know anything about the case. Doctors are either loved or hated, but worst of all they can be resented. Someone resentful could manage to remember compromising details that never took place outside their own imaginations. He knew from his own experience that the testimony of staff members about events in the hospital could range from one extreme to the other, depending on the nature of the relationship the witness had with the doctor. When it was a question of a patient's death, the variations could range from "savior" to "murderer," and the less he was exposed to those kinds of judgments the better. He wanted the cop to hear his point of view as soon as possible—besides, it was the only point of view that really mattered, since he was the doctor responsible for the case—before ignorant staff members started chiming in with their two cents' worth. Really young, that detective, Dr. Nesse thought. He probably didn't have too much experience. He was visibly intimidated by interviewing an older man, especially one more experienced, and a psychiatrist. But he'd still done a good job; he was smart and must have prepared his questions. He'd probably be back with more, under the instruction of Espinosa. He turned off the lights, closed the office, and left.

The traffic on the Ipanema sidewalks was intense at that hour. Ever since he'd moved, he'd avoided taking the car out of the garage at the office. The building where he lived now didn't have enough garage spaces for all of the residents, which meant the parking attendant had to shuffle all the cars every time someone came or went. He didn't want his car shuffled in that way, in a tiny space and by a guy who might not even have a driver's license. He walked home. He'd gotten an apartment that was only five blocks from his office, and since it was so close by he'd managed to get over his aversion to walking through crowds of unknown people. His new apartment, though small, was enough for his needs. The only problem was the garage. Well, it wasn't just the garage. It was also the other residents. They were a little less classy than the people in his old building, but he only encountered them in the elevator.

The sidewalks were packed. Dr. Nesse was struck by how many people were carrying bags. All the bags from shops and supermarkets swelled the volume of each pedestrian to two or three times their original size. There were also delivery people with baskets, boxes, carts, and even bicycles, all gathered there on the sidewalk, not to mention the dogs on leashes. Not to mention the fact that nobody stayed in their lanes, making the normal movement of people almost impossible.

Rua Visconde de Pirajá, Ipanema, seven in the evening. The doctor wasn't looking at the stores. Since he'd started walking from work, he'd never entered one. His purchases always occurred on predetermined days and were almost always conducted over the phone. Of course, he could have taken a cross street, residential, quiet, without many people around, but he was afraid of being attacked. Any thirteen- or fourteen-year-old street kid could fill his chest with a .38 in order to get his hands on his wallet. He preferred the safety of the masses on Visconde de Pirajá to taking his chances on an isolated side street.

His awkward, heavy steps might have made him the center of attention, but nobody was looking at him, or if they were Dr. Nesse didn't notice. He felt like a human iceberg. People often bumped into him. At first it annoyed him, but he soon got used to it.

He turned right, onto one of the cross streets off Visconde de Pirajá. His new apartment was in a building only a few steps from Ipanema's principal artery. Which didn't mean anything. The world was completely indifferent to him.

─────

Welber had left the subway station at the Praça Saens Peña and headed toward the Rua Barão de Mesquita to get the bus that would take him to Grajaú. That distance, which he covered twice a day, was his most urgent reason for needing to get out of his parents' house and into his own place. He'd rent an apartment in the Zona Sul. It could be in Copacabana, Ipanema, Botafogo: neighborhoods that weren't at the edge of the city; neighborhoods where things happened. What was the point of waiting to take advantage of life until he had all the hardware? He didn't want to exchange a stable youth for an unhappy dotage.

The sidewalks weren't so busy at that hour. It was a little after eight and Tijuca was a conservative area. People ate at home—the little family, all together—and watched the evening news and the main soap opera. His parents lived in a small house between Tijuca and Grajaú. It was a quiet area, a quiet street, and his parents' house was a sea of tranquillity. Tranquillity, but not happiness or joy. It was a sad, empty, dead tranquillity. Life there had retired. When Welber stuck the key in the door, his mother got up from her easy chair to serve him his dinner. They ate in silence.

They were finishing up dessert when the telephone rang. Welber got up to answer.

"Welber?"

"Yes, boss."

"Are you eating?"

"I just finished. What happened?"

"Dr. Nesse's younger daughter has disappeared. Her name is Roberta and she's not quite seventeen. The disappearance has similarities to her sister's. I'm at the station."

"I'm on my way."

He caught the bus back to the Praça Saens Peña and switched to the subway to Copacabana. He'd gone from one end of the city to the other in order to eat at home, but his parents hadn't managed to form a single sentence with subject, verb, and direct object, muttering only pleasant-sounding monosyllables. The advantage of going the other way at that hour was that both the bus and the subway were empty. It was a little after nine when he got back to the station. The movement on the streets was still intense. Copacabana slept when other neighborhoods were getting up.

Espinosa was talking to Ramiro, the head of the detectives, when Welber entered the chief's office.

"I was just telling Ramiro about Dr. Nesse's phone call. As soon as he reached home, after you spoke to him, he got a call from his ex-wife saying that their younger daughter, Roberta, had been missing for almost forty-eight hours. She left to go to school and never came back. The mother called all her friends, but nobody had seen Roberta."

"Why did she wait so long to call her husband?"

"Because there'd been a previous episode involving the older daughter, and the doctor's reaction apparently provoked the death of the daughter's boyfriend and the mental instability of the daughter, which she still suffers from. I can understand the wife's reluctance," Espinosa said.

"She already looked . . ."

"Yes. She checked with all the hospitals and the Forensic Institute."

"Could it be that the girl is imitating her big sister?"

"I don't think so. I don't think she'd want to relive the horror of her experience."

"How old is she?"

"Sixteen or seventeen, I'm not sure."

"What solid facts do we have?" Ramiro asked.

"Nothing. No note, no known boyfriend, no useful information from her friends or classmates. Nothing."

"Are we alone on this? Is the Anti-Kidnapping Division aware?"

"There's no sign that she's been kidnapped. Besides, it's a middle-class family, without a lot of money to pay for ransom. There must be another motive for her disappearance."

"Seventeen. She might have an older body and a younger head, to run off with her first boyfriend . . ." Ramiro said.

"It's nine-thirty; I think you ought to go to her house and talk with the mother."

"What's her name?"

Espinosa consulted a note on the desk. "Teresa," he said, copying down the address and phone number and passing them to Ramiro.

"It's right here in Copacabana."

"And the father?"

"He's actually the one who called. The mother didn't know what to do and asked him to get in touch with us. But he knows as much as we do. I think the mother might have a better idea."

Ramiro and Welber avoided stopping in front of the building where Teresa lived with her daughters; the police car, with its shields, letters, and lights, wasn't very discreet. There was no reason to alarm the neighbors. It was a quarter to ten when the doorman announced that two policemen were on their way up.

"Good evening, Dona Teresa, I'm Inspector Ramiro and this is Detective Welber. We're from the Twelfth Precinct."

"Thank you for coming . . . I didn't know what else to do."

"Did you speak with your daughter's friends?"

"All of them. Nobody knows anything. Roberta didn't say anything to anyone, she didn't tell anyone she'd be missing class, and they hadn't heard anything about a boyfriend. There was nothing abnormal in her behavior. Whatever happened to her, happened on the way to school."

"Where is that?"

"In Botafogo. She usually took the bus."

"And when she doesn't take the bus, how does she go, with a friend?"

"No. Sometimes, when it's not raining, she prefers to walk a few blocks to the subway. She might have done that—it hasn't been raining."

"Has your daughter been different lately?"

"How do you mean?"

"Different . . . distracted."

"Inspector, she's almost seventeen—being different and distracted is normal for her."

"Does she talk with her sister?" Welber asked.

"Sometimes. Not always. My older daughter speaks very rarely. Every once in a while they exchange a few words."

"Do you think that she could be repeating her sister's behavior?"

"God, I hope not."

The apartment was completely unadorned, looking more like a cloister than the home of three women in Copacabana. There was nothing extraneous, no decoration, nothing on the walls. There were no rugs and no comfortable furnishings. The only piece of furniture in the room was a round table with six chairs, three of which were shoved against the wall. The only object that worked against the room's austerity was a television that was too big for the room and that seemed excessively luxurious and extremely technologically advanced.

"It's a present from my ex-husband to the girls," Teresa said, noticing the focus of Welber's attention. "It's never been turned on."

"How do you mean?" Ramiro asked.

"Nobody's ever turned it on. We don't watch TV."

"So why did you accept it?"

"He had it delivered here. The kid who brought it over said he couldn't take it back."

"Does he ever visit your daughters?"

"No, it's bad for Letícia, who could have a breakdown."

"Does she have those often?"

"No, but she still takes her medicine to avoid them. The only breakdown she's had since we moved here was when her father came to see her."

"And since then they've never seen each other again?"

"No."

"And Roberta?"

"She used to see him once a week, but then they started seeing each other only once every other week, and now they hardly ever go out together."

"Did something happen to change their relationship?"

"Something happened to him, not her."

"What happened to him?"

"I think he's depressed. He's not interested in anything anymore. He started forgetting to come get his daughter, and then when they went out he didn't say anything most of the time. She started losing interest in seeing him."

"Does Roberta have a boyfriend?"

"She's got friends, classmates, people she hangs out with on the beach, and they're always flirting, but I don't know if she has any boyfriend in particular."

"Does she do any drugs?"

"No. Certainly not. Like Letícia, who'd never taken anything until . . ."

"Until?"

"Until she started taking the psychiatric medication."

"How is Roberta doing at school? Does she get good grades? Has she been in trouble or have you been contacted by any of her teachers?"

"No. Nothing. Her grades are good, she gets along well with her teachers and classmates. Roberta is a model teenager."

"Is her menstruation regular?"

"What are you—"

"Dona Teresa, I have two teenage daughters myself."

"I think it is, but I can't guarantee it. . . . She hasn't mentioned it. Do you think . . ."

"I don't think anything, ma'am. I just think that a girl her age who got pregnant might try to clear up the problem on her own. Not the best idea."

Welber knew how Ramiro conducted interviews: as if he wasn't terribly interested in the subject, leaving the main topic and then returning to it, seeming bored to be there but still able to keep at the game for hours, getting the last drop of information out of the interviewee. When they left the apartment, it was ten minutes to midnight.

"What did you think?" Welber asked when they were back outside.

"We don't have much. The only thing that might be worth checking out is the possibility that she might have had an abortion and things got messed up."

They got to the car they'd parked at the end of the block. Welber took the wheel, and they drove a few minutes in silence. Ramiro leaned his head back against the headrest, but he kept his eyes open. Welber glanced over at his colleague.

"I didn't know you had two teenage daughters."

"I don't."

Welber drove slowly down the Avenida Copacabana. He wasn't driving slowly because of the traffic on the street, which was light at that time of night, but because of the traffic in his head, which was intense and confused, precisely because of the time. It was almost twelve blocks to the station, and he hoped that nothing would happen on the rest of the journey that would require their intervention. Or his. Ramiro was asleep in the passenger's seat. If he only had an apartment in Copacabana, no matter where it was, on the street or in the back, no matter how big it was or what street it was on or who else was in the building, he didn't care, as long as it wasn't in Grajaú, almost an hour away from the station, in that old house that wasn't even his. If he had that apartment in Copacabana he wouldn't have to leave the car at the station and take public transport after midnight only in order to sleep and come back the next morning.

"You're thinking so loud I can hear it from here."

"Did I say something?"

"No, but your ideas are so loud that they woke me up."

"We're almost there."

"No problem, there's no hurry."

"I found out a few days ago that we live in the same neighborhood."

"Tijuca?"

"Grajaú. I don't even know if it's Tijuca or Grajaú, or if it's between them—might even be Andaraí."

"So you live there too. We're both working in the wrong precinct."

"Or living in the wrong neighborhood."

"I'm not sure about that," said Ramiro. "I like Grajaú, or Andaraí, whatever you want to call it. I'm not sure why, but I just like it. I'm not sure I like Copacabana."

Espinosa had left word at the station for them to call him at home as soon as they got in. Ramiro called.

"Chief, nothing solid. Either they're hiding something or the girl disappeared with no apparent motive. Since nobody's demanded ransom there's been no contact with her at all; I'm thinking she had an illegal abortion that somehow went wrong. In that case, she could be dead or hiding at the house of some friend, or with her boyfriend. The mother didn't know if she had a boyfriend. That doesn't mean anything—you don't need a boyfriend to get pregnant."

"How's the mother?"

"In suspense."

"Suspense?"

"Yeah. Like in a movie. I didn't think she was desperate or anguished or sad. She seemed perfectly reasonable, waiting for something to happen. It's strange, but that's how it was."

"Fine. We'll talk tomorrow."

Espinosa didn't suffer from insomnia, but there were nights when he stayed up later than he ought to, of his own free will, with a vague impression that the day still wasn't over, that something was still going to happen.

Most of the time, the only thing that happened was that he lost a few hours of sleep while waiting for his intuition to catch up to reality. He wasn't clairvoyant and didn't believe in premonitions; he just believed that reason and thought worked in silence, for his purposes. And he believed that when reason and logic fell silent, or failed to fill in certain gaps, that was simply a message the listener had failed to grasp. So it wasn't any exterior motive that had him still waiting in the early-morning hours, but his own mind, trying to make itself heard through the clear ideas in his conscience.

Suspense. That was the word Ramiro used. Not anguish but suspense. And he trusted the inspector's acute mind. She wasn't worried because her expectations were positive, because she was convinced that it wasn't a kidnapping. That was the only reason a mother of a sixteen-year-old girl who disappears without a trace wouldn't be tearing her hair out. Another plausible reason was that she knew where the daughter was, and that she knew she was fine.

He considered Ramiro's idea that the girl had had an abortion that hadn't gone smoothly and that she was somewhere recuperating. A few more days and she'd be back. The mother was waiting, but she didn't seem desperate. But then why would she call the police? It's true that she hadn't called herself: it had been her ex-husband. In that case, why would she have warned her ex-husband? If Roberta had had an abortion, the mother's attitude would have made more sense.

He went to the window that gave out onto the tiny cast-iron balcony, but he didn't open the glass doors. It was cold and rainy outside. He stood looking at the square and the empty streets. It was five to one in the morning and he still had on the same clothes he'd worn all day. Except his shoes. He didn't like to wear shoes inside that he'd worn on the street. Not because he was concerned about hygiene but because he liked to feel comfortable and at ease in his house, even when he was alone. He didn't think about those matters too often—it was a little peculiar to devote much thought to them—but sometimes he did. And that's when he understood why he liked thick cotton socks. In the living room, the only light came from a floor lamp next to his reading chair, and that light illuminated his reflection in the glass of the window. It wasn't a very clear image, but it was enough to signal to him that it was time for bed.

Making his way home for the second time that day, Welber went over every moment of the interview with Teresa. One thing stuck in his mind: the woman didn't seem like someone who had just seen her daughter vanish without a trace. She hadn't asked a single question about her daughter's possible whereabouts; she didn't pray for her daughter to return. There was no suffering expressed, only expectation.

The bus left him two blocks from his parents' house.

The dim light that came through the blinds in their room meant that they were watching some movie. If Welber had been home at that hour, the TV would be off and they would be asleep. His mother, especially, had only reluctantly accepted that her son had grown up, just as she'd accepted that he had joined the police.

The room set up with acoustic equipment and protected against external noise by double-glazed windows had been quiet for the last two hours. The only sound was the almost inaudible murmur of the air-conditioning. Even in the winter, Dr. Nesse needed to turn on the air in order to obtain the acoustic isolation he needed for Maria Callas. More than the impersonal and undifferentiated sounds from the street, the sounds from his neighbors' televisions, with their stupid soap operas, annoyed him. He neither spoke to nor looked at the other inhabitants of the building. When he'd first moved in, the neighbors had greeted him, congratulating him on his new apartment. Since he'd never responded to any greeting, much less to any of their commentary, they'd all quickly given up trying to speak to him. When they'd looked at him, their eyes had been fearful. With time, the fear had turned to indifference. Despite his bodily mass, Dr. Nesse had become invisible to the neighbors.

For the last two hours, since he'd come home, he'd been thinking about what he'd have to do in order to, once and for all, get rid of the cops rifling through his life. He hadn't given anyone his new address. He had ended up alone, but there was no reason to advertise his place of exile. Of course, even the thickest cop could take the trouble to follow him from work and find out where he was living. The chief, it was true, had once helped him, and had behaved like a gentleman, but that didn't give him the right to meddle in matters that concerned only himself and his daughters.

He thought about retrieving the articles of clothing scattered around the apartment, as well as picking up the various pizza boxes, McDonald's bags, take-out containers, wine bottles, books, old records, and CDs. Maybe he'd better call back the cleaning lady he'd fired a little more than a month before. But he had no patience with cleaning ladies and he didn't know how to use the Laundromats in the neighborhood. Only when his dirty clothes had accumulated to the point that he had nothing else to wear would he call the dry cleaners and have them pick it all up. Since he never opened the windows, the sickly-sweet smell that dominated his apartment had seeped into his clothes, his hair, and even his skin.

He'd asked for a transfer to an administrative job at the university, until he could decide whether to return to the hospital or resign from public service. The administrative work he did was much less tiring than the clinical work he'd done before, but it was extremely tedious.

Besides, you didn't need to be a doctor to perform that kind of work. Any semiqualified technician could do it. His awareness of this fact often encouraged him to play hooky.

There were still a couple of items left in a box of takeout he'd ordered over the phone. He picked up a meatball and bit into it listlessly. Not even the wine, one of his favorite day-to-day companions, gave him his usual pleasure. In truth, he had so few moments of pleasure these days. He occasionally enjoyed his opera, when the neighbors weren't bothering him, but even in those moments the pleasure wasn't what it used to be—a loss he feared was irreparable. He checked his watch. It was after one in the morning, but he wasn't sleepy; he was just unusually tired, and his exhaustion kept him glued to the chair. He ate out of habit, not hunger. There were still a couple of pastries; he left them in the box.

He was asleep in his chair when the phone rang. He knocked over the bottle of wine as he stretched his arm out in search of the bedside table. It took him a while to notice that he wasn't in bed. He managed to get to the phone only after several rings. There was no voice at the other end of the line. He didn't like repeating "Hello?" into the silence. He hung up. After a couple of minutes, the phone rang again. He didn't feel like playing along with whoever it was in the middle of the night. He picked up the phone and hung it up again, without a word. Seconds later, it rang again. He picked it up, and before he could say anything he heard his daughter's voice:

"Dad . . . something went wrong."

~~~~~~~>

Espinosa considered the winter months, with their blue skies and pleasantly cool temperatures, the best time of the year for walking along the sidewalk by the beach. When he was alone, he preferred Copacabana Beach, a few short blocks from the Peixoto District, but when he was with Irene they chose Ipanema Beach, since she lived in Ipanema. He didn't like to chat when he walked, but he didn't like not to talk when he was with Irene, which inevitably transformed his solitary walk into a sociable stroll. It was pleasant, but different from his own rhythm.

They were both wearing shorts, white T-shirts, straw hats, and tennis shoes, and scarves over their shoulders to protect themselves from the cold wind coming off the water. Even though their clothes were similar, down to the color, the differences were noteworthy. Irene could have been leaving a building on the Upper West Side in the middle of a New York summer, heading to a deli to buy mayonnaise; Espinosa could have been there with her, seemingly integrated into the landscape but fully aware that everyone knew he wasn't a local. Not because of any obvious behavior. But something subtle would give him away, a slight accent: not in his voice but in his being.

"You're very quiet."

"It's just that I don't like to talk when I'm walking."

"I know. But you're 'not talking' more than usual."

"We talked a lot last night."

"No, we didn't. We hardly talked at all. Sex isn't the same as talking."

"Body language."

"When I'm talking, I'm not having sex, and when I'm having sex, I'm not talking . . . except for dirty words. But like I said, you're quieter than usual today. Is something bothering you?"

"Nothing special."

"Anything not special?"

"Do you remember the case of the psychiatrist who committed his own daughter because she was in love with one of his patients?"

"Sad story."

"Absolutely. Now the other girl is missing."

"Was she kidnapped?"

"There hasn't been any contact yet. The girl went to school and vanished. Personally, I don't think it was a kidnapping."

"Why not?"

"Because of the parents."

"What's with them?"

"Nothing."

"What do you mean, nothing?"

"They're not that worried, and they don't seem that interested in the investigation . . ."

"Maybe they're in a state of shock."

"I've seen plenty of people in shock, but that's not what it is. There's more: I got a letter suggesting that the doctor killed the girl's boyfriend."

"The one who disappeared?"

"No. The other one, who got committed and ended up a little nuts. The guy was his patient."

"Shit, Espinosa, it sounds like a horror film."

"It sure does. The guy's disappeared."

"But he didn't die?"

"It seems like he must have, but nobody saw the body. Dead or alive, he completely vanished."

"And what does that have to do with the girl who disappeared?"

"That's what I'd like to know."

"Does she have a boyfriend?"

"A friend said she did."

"Maybe she got involved with an older guy and . . ."

"And?"

". . . and she's spending a few days with him."

"She's only seventeen. Actually, sixteen: she's turning seventeen next month."

"If she's seventeen, she's not a kid. Maybe that's why her parents aren't as worried."

"So why would they get in touch with the police?"

"Just in case."

Espinosa didn't ask Irene to explain. "Just in case" was the kind of phrase that didn't really mean much, he thought, repeating it in his mind. He was so immersed in the little puddle of meaning Irene's phrase provoked that he kept on walking like an automaton, moving a few steps ahead of her.

"What happened? Did you wander off?"

"Huh?"

"Are you lost, dear?"

"I think I am. . . . I mean, no . . . you helped me."

"I did?"

" 'Just in case.' "

"Just in case what?"

"What you said, 'Just in case.' "

"Oh! That helped?"

"It did."

"How nice. So can we go back and take a shower together?"

"I love your logic."

"What logic?"

"*If* your phrase helped, *then* we can go take a shower together. I especially like the conclusion."

Irene's youthfulness could still startle Espinosa. They were more than ten years apart, and to his mind a decade was quite big enough to create a gap between them. That was the problem: how to keep the gap from becoming a yawning abyss. You couldn't get over an abyss, while you could cross, or at least think you could cross, a mere gap. He didn't think that it was a difference in values that increased the distance between them. Values were abstractions. What marked the difference so painfully was the loss of the codes that governed those encounters, mainly encounters between lovers. The codes were perfectly concrete: they could be volatile, they didn't always outlast a single season, but they were real. Either you knew them or you didn't. The years of his marriage, the years he'd spent as a father, his years of family life, and then the years of separation and relative loneliness had made him slightly out-of-date. Sometimes, that made communication with Irene almost impossible. So he fell silent. But silence unaccompanied by thought was simply stupid. That was the silence he tried to avoid at any price.

Including the forty-eight hours that had elapsed before her father had called the station, Roberta's disappearance was entering its fifth day. Espinosa had sent out an alert to all stations, specialized or not in kidnapping cases; he'd circulated a recent photo of Roberta that her mother had provided; and Welber had been sent around to the hospitals and clinics that were known for turning a blind eye to certain laws. Ramiro and Welber attempted to draw a more complete portrait of Roberta, but surprisingly the canvas remained almost blank, though they had a clear physical picture of her. Every inquiry for more solid facts was met with vague replies, or replies that failed to distinguish her much from her sister. It seemed the girl hardly existed in reality, that she was a ghost. Or, worse, the ghost of her sister. And now they were trying to find a real body to match the ghost.

"That's why I was a little uneasy in that house," Welber said, as if suddenly remembering something, when he met Ramiro and Espinosa the morning after his conversation with Teresa.

"That what?"

"Those people in that house are like ghosts. Nobody seems real. The older daughter, who doesn't talk, is a ghost. The mother, from her own account, was always a ghost trying to become a person, except she doesn't know how; with the father it was the opposite. He was the only real figure in the house, but now he's a ghost too. And finally, this girl who just up and disappeared—nobody has any idea why or how—became a ghost herself. And then there's Jonas, of course, who seems to have become a real ghost."

The three of them were in Espinosa's office, seated in a semicircle around his computer. Among the three men there was a connection and a familiarity that allowed a relaxation of the usual formalities governing the interactions of subordinates with the chief. They weren't gathered around the computer to implore the gods of technology to unveil the mystery of the Nesse family. They were there because the room was too small for the three of them and all their equipment to be able to sit comfortably anywhere else. The renovated station had one special conference room, but they were all from the age before computers, back when important decisions were reached in the chief's office, a large space with dark, heavy furniture, steel file cabinets and glass cabinets, pictures on the walls.

Welber's interview with Dr. Nesse added almost nothing to what they already knew. The three believed that until they figured out what had happened to Jonas, they wouldn't really know anything. In fact, they were dealing with two cases of disappearance, in both of which Dr. Nesse played the leading role. It seemed he could be implicated in both cases. Welber and Ramiro emphatically believed that that was a possibility.

"You think he's responsible not only for the death of his patient but also of his daughter?"

"Maybe it seems strange, Chief, but he committed his own daughter; why wouldn't he do it again to the other one?"

"We're dealing with two symmetrical situations. But the signs point in opposite directions: in one he was the victim, in the other, the perpetrator."

"A case of a double personality?"

"Not like in books, but he could, like anyone else, be capable of some extreme evil. Under certain circumstances, an individual who seems good can commit great atrocities, just like people others think are evil can also be capable of great good. I don't think anyone's completely good or completely bad. We're all saints and criminals. Dr. Jekyll and Mr. Hyde aren't just creatures out of literature; Dr. Jekyll and Mr. Hyde are all of us."

"Do you really think that's true?"

"I do. Sometimes you have to protect the doctor from the monster . . . other times, you have to protect the monster from the doctor."

They resolved to let Welber and Ramiro investigate Roberta's disappearance and at the same time check out the information they'd received about Dr. Nesse. Roberta had vanished without a trace; they hadn't learned anything definitive about Jonas, and nothing besides the letter linked the doctor to his disappearance. There was still the possibility that Solange had written the letter, a possibility Welber and Ramiro brought up but Espinosa discounted.

"Two things: the letter is too well written to have been composed by such a low-level employee, and anyway, why would she have written it? Blackmail? If so, she wouldn't have handed it over to the police. To get some professional leverage over Dr. Nesse? I don't think so. He asked to be transferred from the hospital. I don't see why she'd risk it. Unless it was out of love or revenge . . . she was head over heels in love with Jonas. But I don't think that's what happened. You might want to go back and talk to her again."

﹈

At that hour, there were no more parking spaces available on campus, and if they hadn't been in a police car they wouldn't have even been allowed through the gate. They pulled up in front of the reception area, making it clear that they were there on business. Solange recognized Welber and eyed Ramiro suspiciously.

"Hi, Solange, this is Inspector Ramiro. We'd like to clear up a few things about Jonas's case."

"Do you want to talk here or outside? I can ask a colleague to send the patients through."

"Better to talk in a quieter place."

"Jonas's bench is empty," Solange suggested after asking a coworker to fill in for a few minutes.

They crossed the garden in front of the reception area and sat on the bench, Solange in the middle, beneath the mango tree. Ramiro began.

"According to what you told Detective Welber, Jonas used the computer and printer next to the reception desk to type and print the letter that you later gave to the chief of the Tenth Precinct."

"That's right."

"Was anyone else at reception?"

"No. It was already after four, so there wasn't anyone around and the other receptionist had left earlier."

"Do you remember if he had any draft of the text? A piece of paper or notes in a notebook?"

"No, he didn't have a draft. I didn't see anything. He wrote the letter directly on the computer. Sometimes he deleted a part or rewrote it, but it was all straight onto the computer."

"Were you next to him the whole time?"

"I wasn't looking over his shoulder, but I was right

next to him. So if any staff member arrived they'd see that Jonas was with me."

"Did he show you the letter after he printed it?"

"No. I didn't even know it was a letter."

"When did he show it to you?"

"Two or three days later."

"Why do you think he waited so long?"

"I think he was waiting to see what would happen."

"What do you mean?"

"When he wrote the letter, he was already scared that something would happen to him."

"What would?"

"That they'd do what they ended up doing!"

"And what do you think they did?"

"Listen, Inspector, you're trying to get me to say something you won't say yourselves. I'm only the messenger. Jonas was not the stronger party. I'd like to suggest that you look into the people who had some power over the situation. Now, if you don't mind, I need to get back to work."

"Just one more thing. How can you guarantee that the letter wasn't written by you in order to harm Dr. Nesse?"

"Inspector, the crazy people here wear blue uniforms. I wear white."

"But you didn't hesitate to deliver the letter to the police."

"As you said, I *delivered* it. I didn't *write* it."

Solange was standing up, ready to turn her back to the two cops and head back to the reception desk. She didn't seem impatient or annoyed; she simply considered the interview over.

She bid farewell with a gesture and headed back to the hospital building.

"She wasn't intimidated in the presence of cops," Welber said.

"She's used to dealing with crazies."

The notices and photos distributed by the police produced no significant return. Deep down, Espinosa didn't believe Roberta had been kidnapped, though he considered it the best-case scenario. In some ways, a kidnapping was preferable to a simple disappearance. In a kidnapping, there was a certain link with the victim, as well as a high probability that everything would turn out all right. In a disappearance, there was nothing. People disappeared from big cities every day without leaving a trace, and in many cases they were never heard from again.

Since he had nothing to offer the parents, only different hypotheses, Espinosa preferred to say nothing. He wasn't a psychologist but a cop; he was supposed to find out where the girl was, not take care of the parents' feelings. Besides, he couldn't make out any sign of the parents' feelings, at least not the feelings one would normally encounter in such a circumstance. He had the impression that they knew where she was, and that her disappearance was a farce. To counter this impression, there was the fact that they had called the police.

It was a little after nine in the morning when Dr. Nesse came back to the apartment. He took a shower, changed clothes, and left. He wouldn't go to the university. He made the decision as soon as he left home. He had to stop by the office. He started walking toward the Praça General Osório on the same route as always. Even though he walked those streets every day, he remained ignorant of the stores in the area. He needed to stop somewhere to have coffee. Almost all the places he passed didn't have tables; you had to stand at the bar. He needed to sit down. He'd slept for only an hour and he was wiped out.

Two blocks into his walk, he found a restaurant advertising a complete breakfast at a reasonable price. He could do without the reasonable price, since he needed to sit at a table. He was so tired that he stretched out his breakfast much longer than usual. He asked for the check and continued on toward the office. For the first time in months, he had the feeling that he was being followed or observed by someone. He stopped in front of a store window and looked around stealthily. Looking for whom? he wondered. He'd had the real experience of being followed and spied upon by Jonas. But Jonas was a known stalker, easily identified and shaken off. Since Jonas had disappeared, he'd stopped worrying about being followed and had even forgotten that it had happened. And now the feeling was back. It wasn't exactly the same:

there was no well-known figure in the middle of the crowds. What he was feeling now was a still-muted sensation of intensity, whose meaning he knew but whose object was indeterminate. It was no use to look around. Nobody was carrying a sign with the word "stalker" written on it. He walked a little faster. That was the best thing he could do. The walk to the Praça General Osório, even with a long pause, had made him even more tired.

He opened the door to his office and found the rooms plunged in darkness. He turned on the light in the waiting room, looking around for signs of Maria Auxiliadora. Since he had arrived earlier than usual, he figured she could have gone downstairs to buy something or have something to eat. He turned on all the lights. In his own room, on his desk, there was a piece of paper with a message. It was written by hand. Maria Auxiliadora apologized for the abruptness of her decision, but she had to quit. Family problems, she said. In a P.S., she left the phone numbers of two friends, "excellent, nice-looking people, either one of whom could take my place."

Welber had arrived late at the building where the doctor was living. He and Ramiro had arranged shifts of four hours each: he'd stay from eight to noon, Ramiro from noon to four, and Welber again from four to eight. The difference in the number of shifts was the difference between being a detective and an inspector. They didn't expect Dr. Nesse to leave home before eight in the morning. That had happened only when he'd worked at the psychiatric hospital. And indeed, he left after nine, walking none too decidedly, as if he were drunk (which the detective thought highly improbable at that hour) and seeming completely estranged from everything around him. Welber didn't even try to hide. In the state the doctor was in, he wouldn't recognize the detective he'd met in his office a couple of days before even if he should physically run into him. Arriving at the Rua Visconde de Pirajá, the doctor turned left and headed for the Praça General Osório. He reminded Welber of a big polar bear, an animal that, even in the winter, didn't quite go with the Ipanema landscape. After two blocks, the doctor stopped in front of a little blackboard resting on a tripod and then opened a glass door. When the detective came closer, he saw that the blackboard announced a complete breakfast. The doctor was sitting with his back practically to the entrance, which allowed Welber to consider a daring maneuver: his own breakfast had been nothing more than a half cup of black coffee. The detective stayed outside, weighing his chances of entering the restaurant without being spotted by the doctor. He could, naturally, invent a story about the incredible coincidence, but he would then eliminate the possibility of learning where the doctor was going after breakfast. He decided to do the responsible cop thing, and stood across the street, near a kiosk, waiting. After almost an hour, Welber followed the doctor to his office building. No mystery, then, though on the way from the restaurant to the office Dr. Nesse walked more briskly and kept looking around him. He even stopped in front of a shop window, in an unskilled attempt to disguise his real intention, looking slowly left and right and then back across the street. The next two hours brought no news. The most interesting tidbit was provided by the doorman of Dr. Nesse's building: every day, he ordered takeout—pizzas, sandwiches, that kind of thing. That was all Welber had to communicate to Ramiro when he came to replace him at noon.

"He might not have a cook," Ramiro said.

"Or he could be hiding his daughter in his apartment."

"Why? For what?"

"I don't know; it's just an idea that occurred to me."

"A crazy idea. Why would he hide his daughter in his apartment? And then inform the police that she'd disappeared? It doesn't make sense. Besides, the mother would never accept something like that."

Welber shrugged.

"Go to lunch, Welber. When you get back we'll talk."

Standing watch in a commercial building with a large lobby is more comfortable than standing in the street. There was only one entrance, which gave onto the elevator area and the shops located on the street level, five on either side. The shops weren't terribly varied, and there was no bar or cafeteria where he could have a cup of coffee. Ramiro bought a couple of newspapers, sat down on a bench where he could keep an eye on the building, and began the kind of waiting his twenty years in the force had long since accustomed him to. He was still reading the headlines when he remembered the garage. Dr. Nesse could go down the elevator to the garage and leave in his car. He dismantled his observation post and found a place in the square, where he could comfortably watch the garage's exit. It was immediately clear to him that the newspapers were dispensable; he wouldn't be able to keep an eye on the movement of people and cars in and out of a large commercial building while reading all those newspapers.

The inspector didn't think anything would happen until the doctor was done seeing all his patients that day, by which time it would be Welber's shift again. The possibility that Dr. Nesse could lead the cops to the place he'd hidden Roberta was directly contradicted by Welber's suggestion that the girl was hidden in her own father's apartment. Whatever turned out to be the truth, they had to follow the doctor wherever he went.

At four, when Welber came back, there had been no sign of the doctor. In the lobby of the big office building, one man was separating the mail for the various floors and inserting it in mailboxes. He had graying hair and seemed like he'd been there ever since the building was first erected. He greeted the policemen with an indifference that Ramiro and Welber pretended not to notice.

"He usually leaves between six and seven; he only rarely stays later than that. But sometimes he leaves earlier, like today."

"What do you mean, like today?"

"That's what I said. He left quite a while ago. He must have left around two-thirty."

"Jesus! How could he have left if I was sitting here the whole time watching?"

"He left through the pharmacy."

"The pharmacy?"

"The pharmacy over there has another entrance. When he buys medicine, he leaves through there."

The two went out onto the street. The pharmacy did indeed have an exit onto the street, as well as another smaller glass door that gave onto the lobby. Dr. Nesse could perfectly well have gone through that door and left without being noticed. Ramiro made no remark, but his annoyance was visible.

"Let's go to his building."

"Do you think that leaving through the pharmacy was an attempt to get away?"

"Fuck, I don't know, but I'm not letting the bastard escape."

They walked to the Praça Nossa Senhora da Paz in silence.

The doorman said that Dr. Nesse had gotten home around two-thirty. He'd come in a cab, alone, had the driver wait, spent about fifteen minutes upstairs, reemerged carrying his medical bag, got back into the taxi, and left.

The two policemen headed back to the Praça Nossa Senhora da Paz, trying to understand what was happening and trying to forecast his next steps. It was four-thirty. The day was practically lost. Two of the best members of the Twelfth Precinct had been thrown by a doctor who, to one of their minds, resembled a cartoon bear. The temperature had fallen a few degrees. Nothing to bother them. In Rio de Janeiro, though it did get much colder in winter, it never got unreasonably cold, so the jackets they were wearing were more than enough to ward off the city's climate.

Ramiro spoke.

"I have two questions. First, what happened at the office to make him go back home and get his medical bag? Second, why would a psychiatrist need a medical bag? I think the answer is obvious: he needs the bag because he's going to answer a call—not as a psychiatrist but as a doctor. And there's a third question: who called him? It's not so obvious that he's guilty of all the things we're suspecting. It's not clear that the daughter was kidnapped or that she ran away from home. It's not clear that he's guilty of Jonas's death, and it's not clear that he's not. So we don't even know what we're looking for. Maybe we started with the wrong person. And why? Because he was the most obvious candidate."

"Do you think Madame might have something to do with it?"

"I think that before we keep following the doctor, or whoever, we need to know what's really going on."

"Fine. Where do we start?"

"Following the doctor."

"Jesus, Ramiro, you're a real comedian."

"I'm not joking. For once, we'll see what happens; we'll also force him to speed up his plans. You said you thought he looked scared this morning, as if he felt he was being followed."

"And he was: I was right behind him."

"Fine. If he's scared, he'll get even more scared. Let's stick on him day and night. It doesn't matter if he notices. Sooner or later he'll have to lead us to the scene of the crime."

"What crime, Ramiro?"

"It doesn't matter—all that matters is that he takes us there."

It was almost seven in the evening when Dr. Nesse called Espinosa.

"Dr. Nesse, what a surprise—I've been wanting to talk to you."

"Yes . . . sure . . . I've been wanting to talk to you as well."

"Great. Would you rather meet here at the station or in the square?"

"If you're leaving now, Officer, we could meet in front of the station and I'll walk you home. Can it be in about fifteen minutes?"

"Perfect. Fifteen minutes."

When Espinosa went down, he found Dr. Nesse pacing on the sidewalk in front of the station.

"Good evening, Doctor. Any news?"

"No . . . nothing. . . . Have you found anything out?"

"Unfortunately not. My men are working on it, but they still haven't got much. By the way, Detective Welber was looking for you."

"We've already spoken. He was at my office and we had a long conversation."

"After that, Doctor."

"What?"

"After his interview with you."

"Oh, yes . . . whenever he'd like. All he has to do is call."

Espinosa made a gesture with his hand, offering his guest the sidewalk, and they left, walking through the Copacabana night in the direction of the Peixoto District.

"So, Doctor, you wanted to talk with me."

"For two reasons. The first is concerning what might seem my own lack of interest in what's happening to my daughter Roberta. When I called, reporting her disappearance, I myself suggested that my ex-wife would have more to tell than I would. We've been separated for several months, I barely see my daughters, I don't know anything about their new activities, so I thought it would be better for you to talk to her than to me. But that in no way means that I'm not interested in how things are going. And that's the second reason I've come to talk to you today. I saw what happened to my daughter Letícia. It doesn't matter now whose fault it was, because the important thing is that I lost her, maybe forever, and I don't want the same thing to happen to Roberta. I think Roberta ran away from home to go stay with someone. What escapes me entirely is who that someone could be. It's been a long time since she's been seen. I think she's in danger."

"Why do you think she's in danger? If she ran off with someone, it could be that she likes that person. The danger is that she could have run off to terminate a pregnancy."

"That's one of the dangers."

"Do you think there could be others?"

"Revenge."

"Revenge? Whose against whom?"

"I don't know whose, but I know I'm the target."

"Why do you say that?"

"My God, Chief, can you have any doubt? Ever since that worm appeared in my waiting room at the hospital, my life began to be destroyed, almost as if an infection was eating away at the whole organism. Letícia is a limb that's been amputated. Then it was Teresa. I'm scared that it's Roberta's turn now."

"And you think Jonas is responsible for all this?"

"His name isn't Jonas, sir, it's Isidoro. Everything about him is fake. The name is only one of his masks."

"But he's dead. Isn't he?"

"You came to me with a letter accusing me of killing him. That means that for you he's dead."

"And for you?

"I think so . . . I can't say for sure."

"And why would he take revenge on you? For committing him?"

"Maybe."

"Isn't there a motive that predates that? Something more intimate?"

"Sir, Isidoro was a psychiatric patient. That means that he went through a series of preliminary interviews with a specialized team before coming to me. Going through and locating the hidden motives buried in someone's personal history isn't a simple task, not something that can be done in half a dozen meetings."

"Do you mean that he was crazy?"

"You might use that word. I can't."

"You don't consider it adequate?"

"I do, coming from a layman."

"What would be the technical term for Isidoro?"

"'Paranoiac' would be the best, at least as a preliminary diagnosis."

Dr. Nesse walked with difficulty. The sidewalks in these secondary streets of Copacabana were narrow, encumbered by newspaper kiosks and pedestrians headed for the subway station. He was surprised to note that they'd already reached the Peixoto District. He declined the chief's invitation to sit down and continue the conversation on the same bench they'd used previously. There was no need to stretch out the meeting. They bade each other farewell in the middle of the square.

It was seven at night when Welber descended the station stairs and headed for the subway. The sidewalk was empty. In the luncheonette across the street there were few customers.

"Hey, pal, scared of the crowds?"

Before he even turned around, Welber recognized the voice of an old-school detective, one on the verge of retirement but who didn't seem to be in any hurry to stop working. Alongside him was another detective, not quite so old but a lot older than Welber. Despite the hour, and the fact that they were leaving work, they seemed friendly, chatty, as if they were on their way to a party. Welber didn't like either of them, though they'd never done anything bad to him or his colleagues. Apparently, others who worked with them adored them, though true friendship seemed rare at the station.

"We heard that you're looking for shelter here in the neighborhood."

"You heard fast."

"Well, pal, we're investigators."

"More than that: you're psychic. I hadn't told anybody."

"We can guess our colleagues' desires. And we just want to let you know that you can count on us to make your dream come true."

"How do you mean?"

"Listen, pal, around here people help each other out. The life of a cop ain't easy. You can be riding high one day and the next day some little shit fills you full of lead. At that point you'll have your own place, except it'll be six feet under. And what did you have up here? Nothing. What happens to your family? Kids? Damn, buddy, a good-looking stud like you should be getting married soon, having some kids, and then what? Are you going to live with Mommy and Daddy? If you don't get on it, you'll have a pretty sorry old age . . . if you live long enough to enjoy it."

"And what's the solution?"

"You know what the solution is, buddy. We've got a little private mutual-aid society here. Doesn't everyone have insurance? Well, then. We've got something like that. Only it's better. You don't have to contribute every month—other people do it for you. At the end of the month, instead of paying, you receive. It's a safe, guaranteed, risk-free—"

"You're suggesting that I participate in a scheme like that?"

"Come on, man! If you put it that way, you might even make us sound like criminals. It's not a bribe—it's a tip. If you want, we can give it to you as a present."

"I'm not getting involved in that."

"Fine. I don't know what your problem is, but I can guarantee that that's not the way you're going to move along in the world. In any case, if you change your mind, we're here to help you. Your participation in the insurance fund could be very profitable."

"I'm just going to pretend we never had this conversation, okay?"

"Whatever you want, but if you change your mind, all you have to do is pick out your apartment . . . the mutual-aid society will take care of the rent."

The two moved on down the sidewalk, the older one looking up to the sky and stretching out his arm, as if checking to see if it was raining.

Welber sat for a while under the arch of the entryway, watching the two policemen move off after having delivered their message. It wasn't so much a message as a message-invitation, probably kept until they'd figured it was just the right moment to hand it out. It was always the same duo. One talked more, one watched more. Maybe the second knew more persuasive techniques, in case the first didn't manage to close the sale. Every pitch contained both danger and seduction. He had to cut the thing off at the very beginning, before getting trapped in a web of insinuations and half-truths that would be hard to escape from later. He wouldn't mention it to the chief, even though he considered the two cops the scum of the institution. He felt like he could arrest the two of them before he'd snitch on them. That was the way he'd always worked, since his boyhood, a code as indelible as a birthmark.

He headed to the subway station. The trip from

Copacabana to Grajaú included a final stretch on foot to his parents' house through a little subdivision where he'd met Selma during a neighborhood party.

She'd asked him why he put so much mustard, mayonnaise, and ketchup on his hot dog, and he'd answered that a hot dog without mustard, mayonnaise, and ketchup wasn't a hot dog. He could give up the mayonnaise, if she insisted. Selma was the niece of one of their neighbors. She was pretty and had a seductive way about her. Since it was the first time they'd met, Welber didn't know if she was that way with every man or just with him.

"I didn't see you here before."

"It's the first time I've come."

"I'm glad you did."

"How do you spell your name?"

"With a *W*. But it'd be just as ugly with a *V*."

"With a *W* it seems foreign."

They chatted until someone turned out the lights adorning the fig trees all along the wall that separated the little street from the building behind it.

"I think they're trying to tell us it's time to go home."

"I guess they've forgotten that we're grown-ups and can talk until daybreak."

Selma got sandwiches and soft drinks and they went back to the wooden bench they'd been sitting on. Welber noticed that she'd chosen cheese sandwiches covered with some unidentifiable sauce and diet drinks. And she noticed that he'd noticed.

"From now on I'm going to take care of your eating habits."

They still didn't know anything about each other. Neither of them had asked if the other was single—they didn't want to know. Selma's statement seemed to claim him, brushing aside any objections.

That meeting had taken place two years before. Too long ago, Welber thought. He couldn't wait until he had enough money to buy a place of his own; they couldn't keep living with their parents. The solution was to rent a place and move in together.

On Monday afternoon, Ramiro went straight to the station, after visiting the last hospital where Jonas had been seen. He and Welber had lost track of Dr. Nesse since Saturday. The doctor hadn't gone back to the apartment or to the office. He hadn't shown up at the university. Dona Teresa hadn't heard from him. They decided to focus on his relationship with Jonas. Welber had been to Jonas's apartment twice and hadn't turned up very much. The few bits of information he'd gleaned had only made the disappearance seem more mysterious, and they'd bumped up against two difficulties. The first was the double name. In the computers, medical charts, prescriptions, and other official paperwork, he was always listed as Isidoro, whereas ex-patients, nurses, and staff only remembered him as Jonas. When Ramiro compared the written record with people's memories, he saw that few of the facts matched up. The second difficulty was that the clinical team worked shifts, which fragmented their memories. And there was a third problem: a good deal of time had gone by, over three months.

"Chief, everyone refers to him as disappeared or dead, but nobody can say where he died or where the body was sent."

"Is there really no record of his death?"

"There's only a medical authorization for him to have exams in another public hospital. But the other hospital has no record of him. That's it. The psychiatric hospital, the general hospital he was transferred to, and the other hospital he was supposed to go for his exams are Jonas's Bermuda Triangle. His death was only presumed later, in light of the disappearance. But even that was just a rumor, and didn't shed any light on how he might have died."

"He might have been buried as a pauper."

"Or he could have been buried in secret."

"In either event, he'd be dead. The difference is that in the second case there would be a crime."

Espinosa sat alone in his office after Ramiro and Welber left, his thoughts alternating between the two cases connected by Dr. Nesse. He didn't think the doctor was responsible, but he was always turning up whenever Espinosa thought about Roberta and Jonas, people the chief knew only from other people's descriptions. Just now, Roberta was his main preoccupation.

Among the many possibilities raised by the girl's disappearance, one stood out clearly at first, though it fell away with the others until it no longer seemed clear at all. The scene began with Roberta leaving home and walking down the Rua Barata Ribeiro toward the subway station, wearing her blue school uniform, with a sweater thrown over her shoulders, a knapsack strapped across her back. She went past the ticket booth, down the escalator, and walked resolutely toward the platform. That last image, so clear in the security-camera video: but he still had a question. Why, on a cold winter morning, had Roberta thrown her sweater over her shoulders instead of simply putting it on? One potential answer: because she wanted to be easily identifiable in her uniform, and the crest of her school was on her blouse, not on her sweater. And why? Because as soon as she got on the train, she would put on the sweater, which wasn't blue like the uniform but white—and then she'd take a large hat out of her backpack to hide her hair, and carry the backpack in her hand, like a bag. That way Roberta could get out at the next station or, turning around, at the same station she'd entered, without anyone noticing that she was the same person. If that was what had actually transpired, Roberta's disappearance had been meticulously planned by Roberta herself.

Espinosa was used to assigning his fantasies second place. They were frequently very elaborate and didn't always have much to do with reality. He turned off his computer, gathered up his belongings, stuck his gun into his belt, and went out to lunch.

For the rest of the afternoon, the scene of the girl in the subway station wouldn't let go. And his question was this: where could Roberta have gone after she left the subway? There was one hypothesis, which he considered improbable but not absurd: she could have been pregnant and gone to her father for help, even though Espinosa didn't think Dr. Nesse was an understanding enough person for a daughter in need of speedy assistance. On the other hand, Roberta was what remained of his family, and if he lost her he'd have lost everything. And the very idea of a pregnant daughter looking for help from unqualified people could have been a drastic enough scenario for him to try to attempt a family solution. Espinosa thought the idea was a little absurd, except for one thing: the fact that Dr. Nesse ordered, every day, much more food and soda than could be consumed by a single person. Even someone with a physique like his.

At eight-thirty that night, Espinosa and Welber knocked at the doctor's door. He answered on the second knock. He was wearing a dress shirt and a tie, though the outfit, given its dishevelment, had nothing formal about it.

"You . . . I thought it was the deliveryman."

"Good evening, Dr. Nesse. This is Detective Welber."

"Good evening. How can I help you?"

"Can we come in? It won't take long."

"Yes, come in. Sorry about the mess, but I haven't had a maid for over a month."

"Don't worry, Doctor. We won't take much of your time. In fact, what we wanted to know could have been asked over the phone, but since we were right in the neighborhood we thought we'd ask you personally."

"Yes?"

"You said that you usually went out at least once a week with your daughter Roberta. You had lunch together."

"Yes. In the last couple of months it dropped off to once every two weeks. In the last month I think we only saw each other once."

"Why the change?"

"I think it was just regular teenage standoffishness. I didn't worry much about it. I assumed that it would pass."

"Right. And did she usually sleep here?"

"Only two or three times. She was having problems with her mother or sister, I can't remember exactly."

"She'd been having trouble with her sister?"

"In the last few months, I'm not sure. We haven't been living together for quite a long time."

"When she slept here, what room did she use?"

"There are only two bedrooms here, mine and the other, which I got in case any of them needed it . . . even though I was sure Roberta was the only one who would."

"Would you mind if we go check the room out? We might come across something useful."

"The room's a mess. It hasn't been cleaned since the last time she was here."

"For us that's even better."

The doctor got up from the chair with effort and pointed to the hallway. He wordlessly accompanied the officers.

The room held a single bed with a bedside table, a dresser, and a small upholstered chair, in addition to a tiny wardrobe. Though the bed was unmade and two or three pieces of clothing and a backpack were thrown onto the chair, the room was incomparably more presentable than the living room. Of the four drawers in the dresser, three were empty and one contained plastic shopping bags. In the wardrobe was a pair of jeans and a heavy shirt. The room was impersonal, clearly used only for occasional sleepovers. In the bathroom was a toothbrush, toothpaste, and some shampoo; underneath the sink, an unopened box of sanitary pads. Welber carefully examined every drawer and every corner of the wardrobe. He looked under the bed before checking the pockets of the jeans and the backpack, neither of which appeared to have ever been used. The rooms were most notable for their emptiness. During the whole time the cops were conducting their examination, Dr. Nesse remained standing by the door. He made no comment on the obvious lack of personal belongings.

"Thanks a lot, Dr. Nesse. Unfortunately, the search didn't turn up much. Sorry for disturbing you."

They went down in silence and said nothing until they arrived on the sidewalk.

"So what did you think?"

"Imagine you're a fingerprint expert who goes to examine a bus that's just arrived at the station after a few trips, and you don't find a single print. Either everyone in there was wearing gloves, or it was carefully cleaned."

"That's what you thought, too?"

"As for the bedroom, yes. Unless there's one detail we can check out."

"The sweater."

"Very good. Exactly like the one she was wearing when she left home and disappeared. If it's the same one, she was at her father's house after she left the subway."

"It's nine-thirty—not too late to call the mother and ask how many sweaters the daughter has. If she's only got one . . ."

They'd turned the corner and were already out of Dr. Nesse's earshot. Espinosa called the number, which was already in his cell-phone memory.

"Dona Teresa?"

"Yes."

"Good evening, Dona Teresa. It's Chief Espinosa."

"Sir . . . any news?"

"Unfortunately not. Sorry about the time, but I need to ask you something."

"Yes?"

"How many white sweaters does Roberta own? Of the kind she wears to school."

"One . . . I think just one. Why? Did you find something?"

"Don't worry, nothing happened. We're just trying to clear up a few points. Thanks."

"What did she say?"

"She was scared. She thought we'd found her daughter's clothes. We have to be careful with calls like that—people always think the worst."

"What did she say about the sweater?"

"That she only has one."

They walked silently down Visconde de Pirajá. After walking two blocks, Welber asked:

"Chief, we're not looking for the car, are we?"

"No. Didn't we come in a cab?"

"Yeah."

"Who said we were looking for the car?"

"That's what it seemed like."

They got a cab back to Copacabana. Welber got out at the Siqueira Campos station and Espinosa headed for the Peixoto District, only a little more than a block away.

He'd been out since eight in the morning. Despite its cleanliness, his apartment felt a little abandoned. It wasn't that he didn't take care of it. It was clean, and everything was in its place, but it lacked an inhabitant who spent more time there. If he used it only to sleep and bathe, it wasn't more than a hotel room. But he liked the apartment, where he'd lived since childhood: first with his parents, then with his grandmother, then with his wife and son, and in the last ten years alone. He wondered if he himself, rather than the apartment, was uninhabited. He stuck a frozen dinner in the microwave, sampled the leftover wine in the refrigerator, and sat down in the rocking chair in the living room, waiting for the three beeps and feeling much older than he really was.

Ever since she'd separated from her husband, Teresa had reserved an hour every day to walk through Copacabana, heading nowhere in particular, like someone wandering randomly through a foreign city. She longed to get out of the apartment and breathe a little, even if the air was polluted by the passing traffic. It seemed to anesthetize her body and soul. In the last few years, she had forgotten that she was still a young, pretty woman, and that was the idea of herself she was trying to rediscover. She hadn't lost her looks, but she'd lost her charm and her powers of seduction.

When she came back home she went as usual to talk to Letícia. The girl wasn't in her room. She wasn't in the bathroom. She wasn't anywhere in the house. In recent weeks Letícia had been experimenting with little sorties, to the supermarket, to the bookstore, or simply walks around the neighborhood. Teresa had discovered that her daughter took advantage of her own walks to go out herself. She didn't know where she went or what she did, and when she asked Letícia, her daughter replied with silence. She didn't stay out long, never more than an hour. Teresa wanted to believe that her daughter, just like her, was trying out her freedom.

Maybe her daughter wasn't ready for that kind of solo flight. Her hospitalization had left its marks: she was still being medicated, and the pills slowed down her movements and shortened her attention span. Teresa was afraid that she was disoriented. But despite the circumstances, Teresa was still optimistic about any and every attempt her daughter made to break out of her self-imposed isolation. Letícia was young and attractive, though lacking in spirit—the same image Teresa had had of herself when she was walking through Ipanema minutes before. The women in the family were fading away. She went down to the lobby and asked when her daughter had gone out, and if she'd been alone.

"She left just after you did, ma'am. She was by herself. I saw her get into a cab right here."

Half an hour later, Letícia arrived. She'd been gone for more than an hour. Not enough time to catch a movie, but long enough to meet someone. Teresa didn't think it was very likely that she had a new boyfriend, but at the same time she had no doubt that her daughter was meeting someone secretly. If Jonas wasn't dead, she'd bet it was him.

"So, honey, you decided to go out?"

"I went on a little walk."

"On foot?"

"I needed some exercise."

"I think that's a great idea."

Teresa didn't have anyone to talk with about Roberta. Impossible to ask her ex-husband for help: besides no longer being her husband, he'd never been much of a father. Their daughters had been there only to complete the picture of an exemplary family. Even their lunches in the mountains on the weekends, when everyone could share the comfort of their luxury car, were only a scene set up by some imaginary director. She didn't see the point of sharing her anguish with Chief Espinosa either. He seemed like a trustworthy person, but he was a policeman, not her husband or a friend. Girlfriends, she no longer had.

Espinosa's entire day was consumed with taking depositions from people involved in the murder of an elderly couple who had been killed by their own grandson and his girlfriend. Not to mention the prostitute who had laced her pimp's coffee with rat poison . . . and the small detail that the pimp was one of the cops from his own station. The chief wanted to keep the story out of the headlines of the more sensationalist papers, which would have a field day wondering about the cop and what kind of poison the hooker had used.

When Espinosa turned out the light in his office and went down the stairs to the ground floor, it was almost nine in the evening. He was tired and had not the slightest interest in warming up his frozen lasagna. Instead of heading toward the Peixoto District, he turned the corner and went in the direction of the trattoria a little more than two blocks away. Even though he'd lived by himself since he was nineteen and was long used to domestic duties, he didn't like some of them, and the one he savored least was doing the dishes.

On a wintry Monday night, his favorite restaurant would be calm. He didn't like empty restaurants; he liked calm restaurants. He avoided Saturdays and Sundays, when all the living generations of a single family would occupy huge tables, in a spirited contest to see who could talk the loudest and laugh with the most panache. That battle was surpassed only by the challenge to see which table could answer the most cell-phone calls. He liked the idea of a tranquil Italian restaurant where people talked in a civilized tone, which allowed him to ask the owner which sauce went best with which pasta. And while he walked down the little street parallel to the Avenida Atlântica, Espinosa reflected on the pros and cons of the Tartuffe sauce.

The restaurant wasn't, in fact, very crowded, and as soon as he came in he was greeted by the owner, an Italian who had managed to arrive at seventy while still keeping the vigor and enthusiasm of a forty-year-old. He had an enormous joy in discovering new and unexpected combinations for different kinds of pasta. If they were really so new and unexpected, Espinosa couldn't say, but the *patrone* always had an expression of agreeable delight when Espinosa suggested some innovation. So every time he went in Espinosa felt like Columbus, discovering a cuisine that long predated the unification of Italy.

His relationship with food was like his relationship with books: he wasn't an intellectual, and certainly not a scholar, and he wasn't a gourmet either. He didn't like overly elaborate dishes, which intimidated him more than they attracted him; and if he preferred to drink wine with his meals, it wasn't because he was sophisticated but because he enjoyed the mixture of flavors. Since he usually ate alone, he'd developed a palate independent of any culinary orthodoxy. The same was true with books. His grandmother had pointed him in certain directions, when he was still living with her. Since she was a professional translator from English, the authors that he first encountered wrote in that language. He liked his books the way he liked his food: nothing too fancy, but nothing too run-of-the-mill, either.

But while he could count on the *patrone* to help him in matters involving Italian food, he'd lost his guide to literature shortly after reaching adulthood. His grandmother was a quiet, pleasant companion. One day, when he was still a little boy, he was coming back from playing soccer on the street when he saw, from a distance, his grandmother sitting on a bench in front of the building where he lived with his parents (and where he still lived now). He waved at her, but his grandmother was looking at a little handkerchief that she was wringing in her hands and that she kept bringing up to her eyes. Long before he arrived at the place she was sitting, Espinosa understood that he'd lost everything. All that was left was his grandmother. The void that followed a loss like that demanded a strong, fully mature spirit. After another decade, his grandmother died as well. A little less than a year later, he got married, and the marriage lasted another decade. He was starting to think that his life, rather than being measured in years, ought to be measured in decades: the first decade, with his parents; the second decade, with his grandmother; the third decade, with his wife and child. He'd just completed his fourth decade, as a bachelor. He didn't want to risk predicting what the next decade had in store for him.

He left the restaurant telling himself that such thoughts weren't quite what a warrior of the olden times would permit himself, that they weren't appropriate to a contemporary hero, and that they didn't exactly offer a daring philosophy of life.

"I'm not a warrior, I'm a cop; I'm not a hero, I'm a public employee; and I'm no philosopher, despite my name."

The sidewalk was deserted: he could talk to himself. Which, moreover, he'd been doing for a long time.

STORY NUMBER THREE

The doorbell rang insistently, but nobody responded. He soon realized that it wasn't the doorbell but the phone, his phone. He turned on the bedside lamp and groped for the apparatus, which was on the floor, at the foot of the bed.

"Espinosa."

"Officer, I'm so sorry about the time. It's Letícia Nesse."

Espinosa sat on the bed and looked at the clock. One-twenty. He was already entirely awake.

"What happened, Letícia?"

"My mother . . . she's vanished."

"How do you mean?"

"She got a call right before ten tonight, grabbed a coat, and went down without saying anything. She still hasn't come back. She never does that, leaving me alone at night. Something happened."

"I'm on my way over."

Espinosa called the station with a description of Teresa and asked them to search the area around the Rua Dias da Rocha. He left his cell-phone number in case anything turned up. Twenty minutes later, Letícia opened the door of the apartment. She was wearing sweatpants, and there was a coat on the back of the chair. On top of the table, there was a telephone and a little notebook with a list of phone numbers—probably the same notebook where her mother had kept Espinosa's card.

"Do you know who called?"

"No. I was in my room. It was quick, less than a minute. From the way she ran around before she left, I know she was upset."

"Do you know if it had anything to do with your sister?"

"No, she would have said something."

"Did she go out with a sweater or a shawl?"

"She got her coat."

"A purse? A wallet?"

"I don't think so. Her purse is on the bed."

Letícia seemed to be in control of herself. She answered the chief's questions objectively and asked him not to call her father or anyone else to keep her company; she could wait by herself perfectly well.

The phone rang inside Espinosa's pocket. He answered, murmured a few words, and hung up.

"I'm going down to talk with the officer in the patrol car outside. Don't leave here. Here's my cell-phone number in case you need me. I'll be right back."

His colleague's message hadn't been very clear or very positive, and Espinosa didn't want to ask for clarification while Letícia was sitting there. The policeman was waiting for him downstairs.

"Good evening, Chief. I think we found the woman you were looking for, and the description matches. She's sitting on the bench in the square, right over there. She's dead."

"Dead?"

"That's what the lieutenant said; I haven't checked it out personally."

"Where?"

"There, by the newspaper kiosk—you can see it from here. The lieutenant is with the body."

The Rua Dias da Rocha, at the point it intersects the Avenida Copacabana, forms a little square, ornamented by several wooden benches, a kiosk, and a public phone. The lieutenant, a young kid, was sitting on the bench, as if keeping a sleepy Teresa company. He had met the chief on the many occasions when he'd been in the station registering crimes. As soon as he saw Espinosa, he got up and snapped to attention.

"Good evening, Chief. Lieutenant Frota."

"Good evening, Lieutenant. What do we have?"

"A woman who matches the description you sent out. She's dead. I didn't call the ambulance because the body's already cold and stiff, so she must have been dead for at least two hours. I didn't see any obvious wound, but I didn't move the body to examine it in more detail."

"Did anyone around here see or hear anything?"

"Nothing, Chief. Since it's so cold, the night doormen keep the lobby doors closed. They only see what's going on right in front of their entrances, and they can hear hardly anything. There aren't many pedestrians around; people are scared of the cold, and of crime."

Teresa was seated, her hands crossed on her lap and her head resting on her shoulder, as if asleep. There was no sign of violence; her clothes and hair were tidy. She was wearing jeans and a nylon jacket with a wool lining over a T-shirt. She didn't seem to be dressed for a romantic tryst. She wasn't wearing makeup or perfume. She had probably been sitting comfortably at home when she got the call that made her rush out, pausing only to grab a coat.

There was no blood, there was no wound, no marks on her neck or signs of suffocation. Espinosa carefully examined the area surrounding the bench, but he didn't find anything that could shed light on what had happened in that place roughly two hours earlier. But he didn't think it could have been a suicide: people who are about to kill themselves don't get a call informing them about the right time for the procedure and then run out of their apartments in search of a comfortable bench.

Since natural death and suicide seemed out of the question, that left only murder, which implied the presence of someone else on the bench, the author of the crime. The first question was not who but how. Someone with training can break a person's neck without giving the victim time to emit a sound. Even easier if the pressure comes unexpectedly. Another possibility was that the murderer arrived with two cups of hot chocolate, one containing poison . . . or sleeping pills. Shooting, knifing, blows to the head, and other such methods seemed ruled out by the lack of any external signs of violence. Suicide could not be completely eliminated from the list of possibilities: Teresa could have taken poison herself, of her own free will. But in that case, why run out of the house? Could the suicide have been motivated by the phone call? And the poison already ready and waiting? Espinosa asked for the body to be removed to the Forensic Institute. The lieutenant had already isolated the area and placed a guard to ward off curious onlookers.

"Lieutenant, I need to go back to the apartment to speak with her daughter. Call me when the forensic team arrives, please."

It took Letícia a while to understand what Espinosa was saying, even though he got straight to the point. "No rhetoric," he always said to himself before giving news like that. Letícia nonetheless kept asking questions about her mother. When Espinosa finally got through to her, Letícia sobbed convulsively, until she collapsed, exhausted, on the table. A neighbor offered to stay in the living room until the chief could come back.

Espinosa's next step couldn't be delayed. It wouldn't take more than ten minutes to get to Ipanema. It was two-thirty when he rang Dr. Nesse's doorbell; he had to ring several times before the doctor opened the door in socks, underwear, and a dress shirt with no tie.

"Chief Espinosa! What happened?"

"Dona Teresa is dead."

"What . . ."

"She died sitting on a bench in a square, about a hundred feet from her building."

The doctor's first reaction was shock, then fear. There was no sign of pain or sadness.

"How long have you been at home, Dr. Nesse?"

"I got back around nine."

"Did you go out again?"

"For a few minutes, to go to the pharmacy."

"Don't you usually order things in?"

"Only from the pizzeria and the restaurant. I don't even have the pharmacy's number."

"How long were you gone?"

"I'm not sure exactly—I had to find a pharmacy that was open. Maybe half an hour, more or less."

"And you didn't go out again?"

"Sir, are you thinking that I killed my ex-wife?"

"My questions could clear you of any suspicion."

"You asked if I went out again. No, I was very tired, and I took a couple of sleeping pills, which I bought at the pharmacy. I didn't even manage to get undressed."

"Did you call Dona Teresa this evening?"

"No."

"Did she call you?"

"No. How is my daughter?"

"I think she's fine. In any case, you might want to arrange for someone to stay with her."

"I could . . ."

"She asked that it be someone else. I'm sorry."

"I'll get someone."

"Doctor, the body was discovered on a bench on the same street where she lived. I'll need you to identify it."

Letícia spent the rest of the night and the next day with a psychiatric worker Dr. Nesse had called. Espinosa didn't think she needed anyone with psychiatric training; she just needed a friendly someone. But he figured her father, who was a psychiatrist, ought to know what he was doing.

In the twenty-four-hour pharmacy they were able to confirm that the doctor had been there and bought medicine specifically for sleeping, a little before ten at night.

"Can you tell me what he bought?"

"He prescribed it himself: Dalmadorm and Rohypnol. To knock off a body like that you'd need pills for an elephant."

"If he'd taken two Dalmadorms, would he have heard the doorbell?"

"Possibly, but if he took Rohypnol, he wouldn't have woken up even if a fire truck roared into his bedroom."

Dr. Nesse's building didn't have a night doorman, just a cleaner who also kept an eye on the garage, parking and washing the cars, and who came to the lobby if any resident was locked out. He spent more time in the garage than in the lobby. He hadn't seen the doctor that evening.

Back on the Rua Dias da Rocha, Espinosa went through

the buildings on both sides of the street in search of information. It was three-twenty in the morning; the body still hadn't been removed, and the forensic team had just left the area. There was a twenty-four-hour parking place about fifty feet from the scene of the crime, and a restaurant not far from the garage. The only place with a light on at that hour was the guard booth in the parking lot. A kid with earphones was keeping time to the music on his thermos. He hadn't heard or seen anything. A few employees from the neighboring buildings came out to the sidewalk, attracted by the lights of the police cars and an amount of movement uncommon at that hour. But nobody had noticed anything unusual. Nobody had seen an attractive young woman walking alone or sitting on that bench. Nobody had seen a couple seated on the bench either, her head resting on his shoulder as he rubbed her arm. That was how Espinosa pictured the scene.

━━

Espinosa got home around five. He slept all morning. That afternoon he got together with Welber and Ramiro.

"The case has taken a different turn. Before we had an accusation of homicide, but we didn't have a body; now we have a body, but we don't have an accusation. She died between ten o'clock and midnight. When she was found, just before two in the morning, the body was already cold. The fact that she was seated on a bench in a square suggests an impromptu meeting with someone she knew. I don't think that she'd gone out for a tryst. According to her daughter, she left hurriedly and without taking the least care of her appearance. She went out without her purse, her money, or her wallet. Letícia said her father had called that afternoon, arguing with her mother, but she didn't know what the discussion was about. Another explanation for the urgency of the meeting and Teresa's nervousness was the possibility that the phone call was a negotiation for Roberta's handover. Which would have been a possibility, if Teresa hadn't been killed."

"Sir, don't you think it's a pretty big coincidence that a woman whose daughter was supposedly kidnapped would get an unexpected phone call late at night and then a few hours later be found dead on a bench?"

"I'm not thinking about the kidnapping. We don't even know if Roberta really was kidnapped. What we have, concretely, is a disappearance, a mysterious death, and a letter reporting a homicide written by the victim himself, which is just as mysterious."

➤

After eating the pizza he'd ordered, Dr. Nesse went to the window and softly drew back the curtain. There weren't many cars or people around, but he wasn't interested in the traffic: he wanted to know if any cops were keeping an eye on him at night. The experience of being watched by the police was a new one, and he wasn't sure if the surveillance had started only after Teresa's death. He'd had the feeling of being watched before. Actually, it predated Jonas, and went back to the time of his first psychiatric work. He'd always been profoundly disturbed by the stare of a mentally ill patient; it was like the patient could see inside him, running his eyes through his body, examining his every organ, every corner of his physical self; at other times it seemed that patients could see right through and beyond him. It was clear that the man standing all day on a strategic point on the sidewalk was a policeman, as obvious as a postman in his yellow uniform.

He took the elevator down, hoping that the cop would still be watching from the other side of the street. It was a good chance to put it to the test. As soon as he got to the street, he glanced over at the sidewalk across the way. He looked to one side and then the other, scrutinizing every shadow in the buildings, looking behind the trees and the kiosk, but the man had vanished. The doctor didn't bother with his usual evasive routes, heading straight to the Rua Visconde de Pirajá and walking to his office.

For a couple of hundred feet, he didn't feel anyone following him. At night, especially after the stores were closed, it was easier to walk down the sidewalk, but Visconde de Pirajá, even on a winter night, wasn't completely deserted. There was certainly less movement than during the summer, but there were still a lot of people wandering around, making it difficult to pick out the policeman, at least for someone like him, who wasn't intimately familiar with sidewalks and pedestrians and who knew very little about policemen. He walked the five blocks separating his apartment from his office without determining whether he was being followed.

The main lobby was closed during the night, but there was a little door accessing the elevators. Instead of going up to his office, Dr. Nesse headed to the garage. He got in his car and took the exit ramp to the street, pressing the button to open the garage door. Before turning onto the street, he looked around to see if any of the cars parked in the area followed. The Rua Visconde de Pirajá was the principal artery connecting densely inhabited neighborhoods, and in that area there were many restaurants, bars, and theaters, right on the border between Ipanema and Copacabana; it was almost impossible to pay attention to the traffic and still keep an eye out for a possible stalker without running the risk of an accident. He focused on the traffic and put off his concerns about the stalker for a few minutes.

He headed straight to the Avenida Atlântica, where the traffic was lighter, and checked his rearview mirror for cars following him. It was easy enough with private cars, but it wasn't so straightforward with cabs, all of which were yellow and of similar make, though he didn't think it too likely that the police would be following him in a cab. At the time, he hadn't thought about the possibility of a pursuer who wasn't the police. Before he'd gone halfway down the beach, he abandoned the effort. He put in the Maria Callas CD and tried to relax.

When he reached the little square in front of the Duque de Caxias fort in Leme, where Copacabana Beach began, he turned around and headed back. The night was dark and a little foggy. He was halfway through his turn when he was suddenly cut off from the left side and forced to jerk the wheel sharply to avoid being hit, in the process throwing the car onto the sidewalk. The shock of the wheels against the curb stunned him. Everything happened very fast: in seconds, the car and all four wheels were in the square, having miraculously avoided two stone benches. There was no visible damage to the car or to the square, which was empty at that hour.

It took him quite a while before he managed to get out of the car and try to make sense of what had happened. There were no transit police out at night, and no police cars in sight. After a few minutes, he managed to maneuver the car back into the street. There were no witnesses on the street, and he hadn't registered any detail of the other car. The voice of Maria Callas brought him back to the moment immediately preceding the accident. He turned off the stereo and tried to remember how it had happened, but the most he could recover was the shady image of a vehicle to his left forcing him off the road and the crash of his wheels against the curb. He drove for another block and parked next to the sidewalk on the Avenida Atlântica. His hands were trembling so severely that he could hardly turn off the engine. He rested his head on the back of the seat and waited for a half hour, until he felt calm enough to go back home.

He proceeded slowly and carefully, not only because of his fright; he also had to try to piece together the events. Of course, he would have time once he got home, but he wanted to think about it while his memory was still fresh. It might not even have been a car that caused the accident: it could have been a motorcycle or even a bicycle, like that day when Jonas had waved to him. But tonight nobody had waved to him and there hadn't been a bike: no, it was definitely a car. Although on second thought, it could have been a motorcycle. A motorcycle was big, powerful, and loud: it could scare anyone. Just the idea that Jonas could have traded his bicycle for a motorcycle was scary. But of course it couldn't have been Jonas: he was dead. He wiped his sweating hands on his pants and tried to get his handkerchief out of his pocket. The car veered from one side to the other before the doctor got control of the wheel. He decided to forget about the handkerchief. He kept driving, feeling the sweat pour down his face and neck. He reached the end of the Avenida Atlântica, left Copacabana, and entered Ipanema. He went around the Praça General Osório and used the remote control to open the garage of his office building.

Sleep was impossible.

The next morning, he watched the man in gray over-alls clipping pieces of metal to the wheels of the car before raising it off the ground. He didn't really understand what the guy was doing, but he thought it was important to be on hand at moments like that. When the car was raised and the man stood beneath it, the doctor couldn't avoid the question.

"Do you think anything's broken?"

"At first glance, no. But I'm not a mechanic, I only do wheel alignments, so if you think you need a better exam, you should take it to a mechanic."

"It's running fine and not making any noise, but I was told to find a place specializing in alignments."

"Then you've come to the right place. We're the best."

At ten, Dr. Nesse was already in the São João Batista cemetery for his ex-wife's funeral. The burial was slated for eleven and he and four other people, relatives he hardly knew, were sitting in the chapel with the body. At ten-thirty, Letícia and her psychiatric guardian—who hesitated to approach him—arrived. Letícia kept to the opposite side of the chapel. Only the relatives were talking. Letícia stayed awhile by the casket, kissed her mother, and then sat without talking to anyone. A few minutes before the casket was closed, Espinosa arrived, and as the coffin was being carried to the grave, a colleague of Dr. Nesse's from the hospital showed up. A funeral with fewer than ten people.

Dr. Nesse saw his first client at the prearranged hour. Between that patient and the next he had only ten minutes, so he hardly had time to check his appointment book for his schedule for the rest of the day. He needed a new secretary, but he'd have to wait a few days before dealing with that. He couldn't deny that Teresa's death had lightened his mood. He felt lighter, freer. He preferred not to have to keep paying for two apartments, but he was sure that Letícia would never agree to move in with him, even though she still didn't have the means to support herself, and probably never would. The third patient didn't show. Or maybe the annotation was unclear: he'd moved around a few appointments and might have forgotten to write them all down. The answering machine had picked up a call during his previous session, but the caller hadn't left a message; many clients didn't like to speak to a machine. Maybe it was the third client, calling because he couldn't make it. He'd have an hour to confirm his appointments. As liberating as Teresa's death might be, he couldn't fail to perceive that he was in a critical situation. His older daughter had gone crazy, his younger daughter had disappeared, and his wife was dead. Everything had gone up in smoke . . . which was how he was feeling: light as air.

Espinosa was a little disappointed. The forensic team hadn't turned up anything on the bench where Teresa had died, nor had anything been found on the sidewalk surrounding it. The call from the autopsy doctor was just as unenlightening—*causa mortis:* heart failure. That didn't tell him much. But he had told the doctor to tell him as soon as he'd reached a preliminary conclusion.

"Chief, that's my initial conclusion. It could change if something else turns up. The final conclusion depends on the toxicological exams, and that will take a little longer."

He called Dr. Nesse's office. An answering machine picked up. It was three-thirty. He didn't leave a message. He called again at four, and the line was busy. At a quarter to five he got a call. It was Dr. Nesse.

"Chief Espinosa?"

"Yes."

"It's Dr. Nesse."

"How are you, Doctor?"

"Fine . . . more or less . . . not very fine."

"What's going on, Doctor?"

"I'm being threatened."

"Who is threatening you?"

"That's what's scaring me, Chief. It seems . . ."

"Like what, Doctor?"

"Isidoro . . . Jonas . . . the same voice. He said things

that only he would know, things we talked about in therapy."

"Where are you now?"

"At the office."

"Could we talk after you're done with work?"

"Fine. I finish at seven."

"That's fine by me. Could we meet at the usual place?"

"In the square in front of your building?"

"That's right. Unless you'd rather talk here at the station."

"The square is fine. At seven."

➤

Slowly, the story of Jonas's revenge, which Dr. Nesse had told long before, was taking shape, forcing itself into Espinosa's conscience, and that was what he wanted to talk to the doctor about. This latest conversation, however, changed things a little. Espinosa hoped that the meeting would help him define better the person who, though a ghost, was still haunting the Nesse family.

Even before he crossed the street bordering the square in the Peixoto District, Espinosa could make out the doctor seated on the bench they'd occupied during their first meeting. As he came closer, he saw that the man's state had deteriorated even further, and that he looked even more tired and beaten since his ex-wife's death. Dr. Nesse noticed Espinosa only when he was less than ten feet away. He got up to greet the policeman.

"Good evening, Officer."

"So, Doctor, what's going on?"

"Just when I think it's over, something else happens. The story never ends."

"What story?"

"The only one, Chief. There aren't different stories, there's only one. If you'd like, you could call it 'The Revenge of Jonas/Isidoro.'"

"You don't think he's really dead, Doctor?"

"He was. At least that's what everyone thought. It just so happens, however, that the dead man has called me twice."

"Are you sure it was him?"

"I can only be sure when he appears before my eyes."

"And is he planning to?"

"I said I wanted to meet him, and he said he'd call to set a time and place."

"What did he say in the two phone calls?"

"I thought the first one was a prank and hung up. Two weeks ago, he called again, ribbing me for not recognizing his voice. Of course I recognized it. I was so shocked that I could hardly speak. He called to congratulate me on being a grandfather or a future grandfather— I'm not sure which. I didn't immediately understand what he meant, only that my daughter might be pregnant. Since he'd been involved with Letícia, I immediately thought that Letícia was pregnant. As soon as he hung up, I called Teresa. That was when I realized that he hadn't been talking about Letícia but about Roberta, and that Roberta was with him. The son of a bitch drove Letícia crazy and got Roberta pregnant."

"Did he offer any proof that Roberta was with him? Or that he really was Jonas, or Isidoro?"

"He wasn't in the least bit worried about that. He was completely sure of what he was saying."

"Did he ask for anything?"

"No. Nothing. The only thing he wants is for me to suffer. He's not concerned about anything else. He was never interested in Letícia, and he's not interested in Roberta. For him, only one person matters: me."

"And what about Dona Teresa?"

"How do you mean?"

"Did he mention her?"

"Do you think he could be responsible?"

"You would know better than I would, Doctor."

"I never thought he could kill anyone . . . unless . . ."

"Unless . . ."

". . . to make me suffer more. All he wants out of life is to see me suffer. He doesn't want me dead. If I were dead I wouldn't suffer anymore. It's fundamental, for him, to keep me alive. It's not a life-or-death struggle, but a struggle in which one of the fighters slowly mutilates the other, keeping him alive. Alive and mutilated. That's how he's been treating my life and the people I loved the most. First Letícia, then Roberta, and now . . ."

"So he said he'd meet you?"

"He did, as long as it was in a public place. He'll tell me when and where."

"He'll only call you right before, in order to avoid being captured."

"I don't think he's afraid of the police, Chief. To everyone else, he's dead. He's trying to protect himself from me."

"You said that Jonas was taking revenge. What happened between you to create such an intense hatred on the his part?"

"I don't know, sir. If something happened, I don't have the slightest idea what it was. You can't forget that Isidoro is a psychiatric patient, who gave one name when his real name was something else, who disappeared with my daughter for two days, who stalked me through the streets on his bike, who sat day after day in the courtyard of the hospital watching my every move, who had a psychotic episode during one session and attacked me. Isidoro is not a normal person. A person like him can imagine that he's being persecuted, and there's nothing you can do to convince him otherwise."

"But why did he pick on you, specifically?"

"It happened to be me, but it could have been anyone. His persecutor is imaginary; it's a kind of personality that he could project onto anyone close to him."

"Do you think he's capable of murder?"

"Now I do."

"I'm going to leave two of my best men on guard for when he arranges the meeting with you. Don't worry about the time: you're going to call these numbers and tell us where the meeting is going to take place. If he wants to see you immediately, make an excuse and ask for another half hour."

"Chief, don't forget he has my daughter."

"I can only hope he does, Doctor."

<hr />

While he was heating up a spaghetti Bolognese, Espinosa thought about how the portraits he'd initially drawn in this case had become blurrier and blurrier, not because more time had passed but because the surface of each one had changed. Every time a mask was removed, the result was not a more genuine face but simply another mask. Yet that was what he expected. He had never deluded himself into believing that you could ever get down to the real face.

Some relationships in the case didn't make sense. If the aim of Jonas/Isidoro was to get Roberta pregnant, why did he need to kidnap her or convince her to run away from home? It would be easier, more comfortable, and even more cruel, if that was what he truly wanted, to let her pregnancy flower in the Nesse home. Unless . . .

The three beeps from the microwave announced that dinner was ready. Since his last bottle of red wine had been consumed days before, he had to make do with a can of beer.

. . . unless that was exactly what had happened. Roberta had gotten pregnant and stayed home without saying anything to anyone. She'd waited until any attempt to end the pregnancy had become dangerous. If this was how it had played out, where was she now? And why hadn't she come to her mother's funeral?

It was too early to go to sleep, too late to go to the movies, and he didn't feel like seeing anyone. He'd been trying, for a while now, to substitute novels for short stories. With the life he led, he couldn't allow himself the time that reading a good novel demanded. He usually took up a novel again only to realize that he had no idea what had happened before, or had forgotten what such-and-such a character was doing there. Short stories had the advantage of being consumed in one sitting. It was true that he'd already forgotten what he'd read a couple of stories before, or even what the last one he'd read was about, but he wrote that off to fatigue.

He closed the windows in the living room but opened the blinds in order to see the lights on the hills above the neighborhood. He sat down in the rocking chair, turned on the lamp, and took up his book again. The telephone didn't ring, the doorbell rested silently, the cell phone kept quiet. But he couldn't read a whole story. Roberta was more present than the book. There was something in Dr. Nesse's story that didn't sound quite right. Or maybe that wasn't it, but several things, different things, that were off. Maybe that was the problem: too much information. There were several different stories, each of which made sense, but together they didn't all add up. Every time a new fact appeared, the picture became fuzzier.

The story the doctor had told about Jonas made perfect sense, but in conjunction with the other stories it didn't match, any more than it matched the reports other people had given about Jonas. The idea that Roberta had fled in order to be with Jonas might make sense on its own, but it had nothing to do with a relationship between Roberta and Jonas, which nobody had suspected. The disappearance of Jonas himself, after his transference from the hospital, could have happened without Dr. Nesse's intervention, although it didn't match up with Jonas's letter. And Teresa's death didn't match up with anything.

He got a notepad and made a series of notations, numbering each of them, like a group of propositions. After reading and rereading them all, Espinosa drew a series of diagrams, little rectangles with names inside them, which connected to other rectangles, forming a web. The first web was very intricate, and slowly the scheme began to look more organic. It was early in the morning when he left the rocking chair and got into bed.

Among the Post-it notes he found on his desk, one asked him to call Dr. Marcos at the Forensic Institute. Before he called, Espinosa got another cup of coffee from the machine. Together with the cups he'd had at home, it was enough caffeine to raise the dead. Which was what he hoped for from Dr. Marcos.

"Good morning, Doctor. I got your message."

"Chief, I think we've got something on Dona Teresa. It took me a while to tell you because I had to check it against some other tests."

"Yes, Doctor."

"She had taken a good amount of flunitrazepam. The commercial name is Rohypnol, a.k.a. 'Good night, Cinderella.' No problem there—it was at night and she might have had trouble sleeping, but it so happens that I also found a surprising quantity of potassium chloride. Between fifty and seventy milliliters."

"What does that mean, Doctor?"

"It means that nobody has that much potassium chloride in their body unless it's been put there deliberately."

"And?"

"And she died of cardiac arrest."

"That's what you told me before."

"That's right. And I was correct."

"So what's the problem?"

"The problem is that a young, healthy woman with no history of heart disease doesn't suffer cardiac arrest because she sat on a bench at night to flirt. The potassium chloride, if injected in the proper amounts, provokes immediate cardiac arrest."

"So you're saying someone poisoned her with potassium chloride?"

"That's what I'm inclined to think. Unless, of course, she'd taken it herself. There was a mark of a recent intravenous injection in her arm."

"There was no syringe, nothing, that was found near her in the street. Could she have injected it and then gone to——"

"No. Death is immediate. She wouldn't have had time to throw away the syringe and then come back to the bench. She wouldn't have even had time to get rid of the syringe by throwing it somewhere."

That closed a series of circuits in the diagram he'd been drawing the night before. The whole thing was starting to make sense. He called Ramiro and Welber into his office.

"It was murder."

"Teresa?"

"I just talked to the doctor who did the autopsy. The cardiac arrest was brought on by the injection of potassium chloride."

"No doubt?"

"No doubt. She had more than the necessary amount to cause death."

"How could someone do that without her reacting?"

"He also found a good amount of flunitrazepam. The commercial name is Rohypnol."

"'Good night, Cinderella.'"

"Exactly. Either she took the sleeping pills before she got the call, or she must have drunk something with the medicine in it. Once she was asleep, the murderer could even choose a place where the mark wouldn't be very visible."

"Dr. Nesse? He'd bought Rohypnol that night, remember?"

"Anyone can administer an intravenous injection; you don't have to be a doctor."

"But not everyone knows that potassium chloride kills."

"But anyone can find out. Now, for example, we know, and we're not doctors."

"So are we going to squeeze Dr. Nesse?"

"No. We're not even going to let him know about the medical report. I want to determine one thing first. When we looked for dead vagrants, unknown people with the same physical characteristics as Jonas, we only looked at the bodies that went through the Forensic Institute. Now I want you to check out the deaths that occurred in hospitals. When someone like that dies in a hospital, the presiding doctor attests to the *causa mortis*. The body doesn't even go through the Forensic Institute. I want you to check in the emergency rooms of the main public hospitals on the day Jonas left to get his exams. Ignore women, old people, and children. I want you to look at the deaths of young white men buried as paupers. There can't be too many of them."

His lunch was a Big Mac with fries and a milk shake, his fattier alternative to spaghetti and red wine. The afternoon passed without much news until five-twenty, when he received a call from Dr. Nesse.

"Chief, he called!"

"Who called?"

"Isidoro, Jonas, we arranged to meet at six in the Praça General Osório, here across the street. He wanted it to be immediately, but I said I was with a patient. I didn't manage to find the officers you told me to get in touch with."

"They're on duty. I'll be there. Did you specify any place in the square?"

"He told me to keep walking down the sidewalk, that he'd find me."

"Fine. If you see me, don't make any gesture or keep looking at me. And don't do anything yourself: leave everything up to him."

~

The detective available was Chaves, a rookie, clever but still inexperienced. Espinosa explained what was going on, gave him clear, detailed instructions, and the two took a taxi to the square. They waited inside a newspaper kiosk in front of Dr. Nesse's office. As soon as Espinosa saw the doctor come outside, he identified him for Chaves and the two split up. It was five to six. Jonas had never seen the two cops, so they didn't need to hide.

Dr. Nesse was doing everything possible to remain calm. The result was a large, nervous man pacing from one end to the other of a very busy sidewalk. Six o'clock. While Chaves strolled down the same sidewalk, Espinosa surveyed the scene from the other side of the street, which afforded him a clear view. At six-twenty,

Dr. Nesse crossed the street toward the policeman, holding a piece of paper in his hands.

"A kid walked by and handed me this."

It was a regular piece of paper, torn in half and a little rumpled, with the phrase "YOU TOLD THE POLICE" written in block letters. The doctor was still just as nervous as before and looked at Espinosa as if awaiting a magic spell that would transform the situation.

"Doctor, you'd better go home. You said that he was the one who contacted you, which makes us think that he wants to meet you. We'll wait. He'll certainly try again."

Chaves was crossing the street. They got in the first taxi.

"I didn't see anyone come up to him, sir."

"He said it was a kid."

"I didn't see any kid. It's true that he was in the middle of a lot of people and that one of them could have given him the note, but I don't remember any kid."

The next morning, Saturday, Espinosa called Letícia to arrange a meeting. He didn't want it to be in her apartment, where everything recalled her mother, and he didn't want it to transpire in front of the guardian sent by her father. Only when Letícia opened the door did Espinosa invite her to have breakfast in one of the hotels on the Avenida Atlântica. The guardian started to gather her coat and purse, but Espinosa made a gesture with his hand.

"Don't worry, I'll take care of her. We won't be more than an hour. You could go out or rest a little."

The woman didn't respond, but she didn't seem to approve of the officer's initiative. Of course she would call Dr. Nesse immediately to tell him, but neither Espinosa nor Letícia was very worried about that. Espinosa suspected that the psychiatric guardian was more of a watchdog appointed by her father than a helper, though he was aware that Letícia was in no position to live by herself.

Letícia was visibly relieved by the invitation. They left arm in arm, turning to the left on the Avenida Copacabana and then right onto the Rua Santa Clara, toward the Avenida Atlântica. It was only four blocks, and the morning was pleasant. They chose a hotel with a terrace on the beach and ordered a full breakfast for two. It was fifteen minutes to ten.

"I've already eaten, but I love hotel breakfasts, especially with a view like this."

"I have too, but it will be a little pre-lunch."

"Thanks for getting me out of that apartment and away from that woman for a while. She's not a bad person, but she views everything very suspiciously and, of course, gives my dad a detailed report of my every move. But for now it's better than being alone there."

"Does your father still medicate you?"

"He still sends the medicine."

"And?"

"For the last few months, I've kept reducing the dosage until I stopped completely. For the last two months I haven't taken anything. At the end of every day, I count out the prescribed amount and toss it into the toilet. That way it runs out on the expected day."

"And how do you feel?"

"I'm getting along. Mom's death was the worst thing that ever happened to me. She was all I had left. In six months, I lost my boyfriend, my sister, and my mother. What do you expect? If I'm sitting here with you and enjoying the view, it's a sign that I still have a little sanity left."

"Why does your father keep sending you medicine?"

"Because he needs to keep me dependent, and he can only do that if I'm doped up."

"And he doesn't notice that you're not?"

"No. I pretend. I know how it feels."

"But doesn't he want you to recover?"

"Recover from what?"

"From what you had."

"What I had was pain and sadness. Neither of those is a sickness."

"So why . . ."

"That's how he controls reality. With drugs."

"And how long are you going to keep pretending?"

"There's no more need for me to do it. I've lost everything I could lose. I'm trying to regain a little autonomy.

In the last few months, I took advantage of when my mom went out to go out as well. I needed to reassure myself that the world was still there. I thought about going to medical school, but now I've changed my mind. I'm going to study literature. I don't have any idea how I'm going to support myself: I need to get a job, I don't want to be dependent on my dad. But the problem is, I haven't been able to make new friends. In some ways, I'm still locked up in the hospital."

"What do you think happened to Jonas?"

"I think he died."

"You never heard from him again?"

"Never."

"Why do you think he died?"

"If he hadn't, I'm sure he would have gotten in touch with me."

"Do you know about a letter accusing your father of being responsible for his death?"

"I haven't read the letter, but I know it exists."

"What do you think about it?"

"My father hates Jonas. It doesn't matter that he's dead: he hates him just the same. I don't know why—he never explained it to me. But whatever the reason is for his hatred, I don't think that my father would go so far as to kill him . . . or I don't want to believe that. It's very hard for me. But I can see that he might have indirectly caused my boyfriend's death."

"What do you think happened to your sister?"

"I think she couldn't stand the pressure."

"What pressure?"

"From my father. You have no idea how authoritarian he is. It can get unbearable, and my sister is a very sweet person—she doesn't know how to react to that kind of oppression."

"When you say she couldn't stand the pressure, do you mean she fled?"

"I think she hid from our dad."

"Why? Did he have something against her?"

"No, to the contrary. She was the only one of us who still got along with him."

"So why, then?"

"Maybe something had happened that he couldn't accept."

"Do you think that your mother knew where she was hiding?"

"I think so."

"Of course, without your father suspecting anything."

"If my father suspected . . ."

"If he suspected . . . ?"

"I don't even know what he would do."

"Would he attack your mother?"

"He doesn't do anything halfway. Either he's very nice or he's very mean. Attacking people isn't part of his repertoire."

"And when he's bad . . ."

". . . he's very cold. When we still lived together and he started feeling stalked by Jonas, he showed up one day with a revolver. He said it was for self-defense, in case he was attacked. Of course my dad didn't need a gun to defend himself from Jonas: he's almost twice his size and could easily kill Jonas with his own hands, but he would never do that. He needs death to be antiseptic, like in the hospital. So the gun . . . he kept it in the wardrobe and never brought it out again."

"Jonas never explained in more detail what had happened between him and your father?"

"Jonas didn't talk about his own life. He didn't like to dwell on the past. Do you like literature, sir?"

"If we're going to talk about literature, you can't call me sir."

"How nice. . . . Do you like literature?"

"I do."

"Tell me one author you like."

"Conrad, Melville, Hammett . . ."

"Are you married?"

"I was. But if that's a proposal, I think you'll be better off if we stay just friends."

Espinosa thought that Letícia was doing her best to avoid the main question of that meeting, and he didn't want to be the one to force it. Besides, the girl seemed to be enjoying one of her few pleasant moments of the last couple of months. They kept talking about authors and books. The complete breakfast was duly appreciated, with plenty of food to go around. It was only when they were on the sidewalk, heading back to the apartment, that Letícia finally popped the question.

"Espinosa, what happened to my mother?"

"She had cardiac arrest."

"Everyone who dies has cardiac arrest."

"Well, that's what she had."

"Espinosa, was it brought on by natural causes?"

"No, it was brought on by an excess of potassium chloride in her body."

"Potassium chloride? Was she sick?"

"No, it was injected."

"Accidentally?"

"That would be difficult. It was injected right there. Death was immediate."

"How could that have happened?"

"The doctor who did the autopsy says that potassium chloride has to be diluted in a serum and has to be applied with something called a scalp: a little bottle of serum and a syringe."

"Was it suicide?"

"No."

"So . . . someone . . ."

"It's possible."

"But who? How did she let someone inject it into her?"

"Besides the potassium chloride, the toxicologist found a substance called Rohypnol. Do you know if she took any medicine before she went out?"

"I don't know. I was in my room. Do you think she could have taken the medicine and then . . ."

"The Rohypnol, yes, but she couldn't have injected the potassium chloride herself."

"So she was murdered. Is that what you're telling me?"

"That's what the facts suggest. But the investigations are only preliminary. We have to find out who did it, how, and why. I still don't have an answer for any of those questions."

Ramiro and Welber spent the day checking out the hospitals where Jonas might have been sent for exams. They focused on the busiest hospitals, checking the records for the day he disappeared. It was no use searching under the name Jonas or Isidoro. They looked for a white male patient, between twenty and twenty-five, of unknown identity. That was all they had—not the most useful information, but not entirely useless. There were only a few candidates. For the day Jonas had left the general hospital, they found only one death certificate, for a death that occurred at the end of the afternoon. It was a man of unknown identity whose physical characteristics corresponded to Jonas's. They also discovered three other deaths in the two days following that might have been Jonas. But only the first one was a perfect match, and the body had been buried in a canvas-and-wood box, in a shallow pauper's grave. A coffin like that, buried during a rainy summer month: there was little hope that they could identify a body interred in such conditions, months earlier.

"Where was he buried?" asked Espinosa.

"In the cemetery of Pechincha, in Jacarepaguá."

"While I get the authorization to exhume the body, try to find exactly which grave it is. I'll do what I can to get the okay by tomorrow. When they exhume the body, you might not find anything that allows an immediate identification. You'll have to try to find some detail that may be a clue."

———

Over the next two days, Welber and Ramiro learned that it wasn't easy to locate and disinter a five-month-old cadaver, and that the grave diggers didn't rush to help out.

"Just think, what if we started digging up everyone we've already buried?"

"Don't worry, that's not going to happen. Besides, we'll buy you a nice cold beer after you're done."

Of the coffin, only a part of the wood frame remained. The two cops rubbed their noses with Vicks and made a preliminary evaluation of the body, or something that a few months before had been a body and now was bones and remains of clothes and muscles. The size could be a match, but it was impossible to recognize the face. There was no face. That said, they could see that the body had black hair. They called the chief.

"Get the death certificate or the report from the hospital where the man died."

"We have the death certificate. It describes the characteristics of the dead man, identity unknown, and that the man died before he could be treated by a medical team."

"And the cause of death?"

"The only thing it says is cardiac arrest."

Espinosa asked the forensic team what tests of the bones and hair could reveal. He learned that the presence of potassium chloride could be detected, but that this substance could be found in almost all the bodies buried in the paupers' section of Pechincha, a cemetery located in a potassium-rich soil.

The facts—that the unidentified person buried as a pauper had died of cardiac arrest when he wasn't quite twenty-five years old, and that the person had been removed from the same hospital where Jonas was last seen, and on the date when he was reported to have disappeared—were more than enough for Espinosa to consider seriously the possibility that the body belonged to Jonas, or Isidoro. The problem was that Jonas/Isidoro didn't use a last name, that the names of his parents were unknown, as were his place and date of birth, identity card number, fingerprints, confirmed address, relatives, or friends. He hadn't had a legal existence. So legally he hadn't died.

Ramiro and Welber were satisfied with the result of the search and frustrated by its uselessness from a legal perspective. But they had known beforehand, just as Espinosa did, that this would be the case. They were searching not, as they usually did, for objective proof but for subjective certainty.

"Chief, there's no doubt it's him: same height, black hair, same date . . ."

"Our problem is: who?"

"Jonas, of course!"

"And who's Jonas? We don't even have a picture of him. All we can do, at the most, is point to that heap of human remains that you found in the cemetery of Pechincha and say: those are the mortal remains of a man whose name we think is Jonas, but about whom we don't know anything else. He's unidentifiable. The man you found, according to the hospital records, died of natural causes. It doesn't say what the causes were, only that his heart stopped beating. What can we do with that? Open a criminal case? Who killed whom?"

"So we're going to write it all off?"

"I didn't say that. I just said that there's no way it would hold up in court. But we can use it for ourselves. I'm not going to write off our conviction that the body is Jonas's, whoever Jonas may be. I wouldn't write off the fact that this Jonas died of cardiac arrest at age twenty-two, which is pretty unusual. I haven't forgotten that Dona Teresa also died of cardiac arrest, and that her death wasn't natural. And I'm not forgetting that Dr. Nesse has said that Jonas is stalking him. So either the body we found is Jonas's and Dr. Nesse is lying, or Jonas really is stalking Dr. Nesse and in that case the body belongs to someone else and we're completely wrong about everything."

Espinosa considered it strange how the emphasis in the case kept shifting. At first, the emphasis had been on the letter, pointing the finger at Dr. Nesse; then it was the disappearance of Roberta; then the death of Teresa; finally, it was Dr. Nesse claiming to be stalked by Jonas.

The intriguing part of the story was that everything following Jonas's disappearance had been reported by the doctor. Nobody ever saw Jonas threaten anyone. To the contrary: all the descriptions were of a calm, polite person, nothing like the aggressive young man Dr. Nesse described. Even the revenge the guy had ostensibly planned had never been confirmed by anyone, or put into practice in any visible way. The stalker Jonas/Isidoro could have been a psychiatric patient threatening the doctor's family, or he could have been someone the doctor himself had imagined.

The next evening, as Espinosa was trying to decide between lasagna and cold cuts, the phone rang.

"Espinosa?"

"Yes?"

"It's Letícia."

"Letícia, how nice to hear from you. How are you?"

"Not too great . . ."

"What happened?"

"I didn't tell you everything. I hid something . . ."

"You didn't tell me everything when?"

"At breakfast in the hotel."

"Listen. It's eight-thirty. I still haven't had dinner. There's an Italian place almost next door to your building. The pizza's good. We can eat while we talk."

"Fine . . . without my guardian."

"Of course. I'll see you on the terrace in twenty minutes."

It wasn't a very cold night, but Espinosa preferred the inside of the restaurant to the sidewalk terrace. On reflection he realized the choice of restaurant might not be ideal: it had the advantage of being close to her building, but it had the disadvantage of being too close to the place her mother had been killed. Letícia arrived with the guardian, who left her in Espinosa's care.

"Sir, will you please bring her back to the apartment after you're through?"

"Certainly."

Letícia greeted Espinosa with two kisses on the cheeks and an attempt at a smile, inadequate to mask her sadness. In the little room on the second floor of the building, there were a half dozen tables, two of which were occupied. They chose the most private table.

"Do you like pizza?"

"I do, but I'm not hungry."

"We could get a pizza and a couple of glasses of wine. We can nibble at it while we talk."

"Fine."

"So? You said you weren't very well and that you hadn't told me everything in our last conversation. I think it's perfectly normal that you don't feel well; it would be strange if you did. As for not telling me everything . . . nobody tells everything."

"But I didn't mention something that could be very important."

"And you feel like telling me now?"

"Not really . . . but I need to. Nothing's clear: they're just impressions mixed with facts."

"Tell me, without worrying about getting it exactly right."

"Some of these impressions have to do with recent events, others with things that happened six months ago. My idea of time was a little mixed up when I was taking the pills. My memory as well. The older memories, from when I was being medicated, are the least precise—I'm not sure how seriously I ought to take them, actually; but they have to do with Jonas's disappearance.

"Here's what happened: nobody questions that the person directly responsible for committing him and then transferring him was my father, so that's why they blame him for Jonas's death. I don't think everyone's taken seriously the possibility that my dad might have, himself, literally killed my boyfriend, but shortly after the news of Jonas's death I heard a phone call between my parents about the pills my dad was forcing me to take, in which my mom said, 'You already killed the kid, now you want to kill our daughter?' At the time, I under-stood the phrase 'You already killed the kid' to mean that my dad had been indirectly responsible for his death, which, in any case, was what everyone thought. I didn't pay attention. Then the months went by and there were all these changes in our life—and then Roberta disappeared. I hadn't been taking the pills for months, my parents had separated, we were all less submissive and more emotionally independent. I didn't know what had happened to my sister, but I knew it was all very strange. Neither my father nor my mother was really worried or interested in what the police were doing. Besides, they talked on the phone every day, and the conversations almost always ended in shouting matches. The last one was earlier on the day Mom died. In that fight, I heard everything Mom said because she was yelling at him. I clearly heard the phrase that reminded me of what she'd said months before: 'You almost killed Letícia, and now you want to kill Roberta? I swear that if anything happens to my daughter I'm going to the police!' That wasn't the only thing I heard but that was what stayed etched in my memory. . . . I don't think I'll ever forget it."

Neither of them had touched the pizza or the wine that the waiter had placed on their table. Espinosa noticed Letícia's effort to maintain her composure, but he had no doubt she was on the verge of a meltdown.

"How about a slice of pizza and some wine?"

"Okay . . . a little wine . . ."

Espinosa waited for her to take a few sips of the wine. He told her that when he was a boy he'd had a few friends who lived on this street, and that one of them had lived in the same building where they were now sitting. He used to walk from the Peixoto District, only about three blocks away, to play ball in the street. Sometimes it was the other way around: they went to play in the square of the Peixoto District, unpaved, where no cars passed, and which more closely resembled a soccer field. But since he was in the minority the game usually happened on the Rua Dias da Rocha, which at that time still went through to the Avenida Copacabana, though it was unusual for the game to be interrupted by a passing car. He also talked about the Cinema Metro and his Sundays spent watching Tom and Jerry, and recalled the first time he went to the beach alone. Espinosa saw the stress slowly melting off of Letícia's face, and she appeared more relaxed.

"Espinosa, do you think I should take the conversation I heard literally?"

"You didn't hear a conversation; you just heard your mother talking. Are you sure she was talking to your father? Did you hear her say his name? The words could have been spoken to Jonas."

"Jonas?"

"I'm not saying she was talking to him, just that the contents of what she said could have applied to him as well."

"But . . . that's crazy . . ."

"It might be improbable, but it's not crazy. When you heard your mother say, months ago, 'You already killed the kid, now you want to kill our daughter,' the verb 'kill' could have been used in a less-than-literal sense—she could have been talking about the effect the medicine had on you, and the fact that Jonas was also being medicated by him."

"She wasn't talking to Jonas! Jonas died! I know how she talked to my father. She was talking to him, not Jonas!"

"Letícia, I'm not saying she wasn't talking to your father. I'm just saying that from what you overheard, she could have been talking to someone else. It could have been your father or it could have been someone else, even though I know that for a long time he'd felt persecuted by Jonas and that that feeling could have taken on more dramatic proportions. I also know that he saw Jonas as the embodiment of evil, someone whose only goal was to destroy his family, and that feeling seems to be back in full force. He says he's being stalked by Jonas *now*, that Jonas wants to set up a meeting with him. . . . He could be lying, he might have gone crazy, but he could also be telling the truth. I'm only trying to say that despite all of this, from what you heard, she could have been speaking to someone else besides your father. It's very improbable, but it's not impossible."

"But Espinosa, Jonas died!"

"Did you see him die? Did you see the body?"

"Everyone knows it!"

"It's not true that everyone knows it. People only *say* that he died. Nobody saw anything or has any proof whatsoever that he actually died."

"Do you think . . ."

"What I think doesn't have anything to do with it. We're just guessing. Speculating. There's no irrefutable proof of Jonas's death."

"Espinosa, I know very well how my mother talked to my father and I can guarantee that she was talking to him, and not to Jonas or some other person. That's not speculation. My mother's death is not a speculation or a guess."

"Of course not."

"And what about what she said about Roberta? About Dad being able to kill her?"

"It might have been metaphorical."

"And what if it wasn't?"

"Why would he kill Roberta?"

"Out of desperation . . . accidentally . . . I don't know. I can't think about that."

"Did you ever hear your mother suggest that Roberta was with your father? Did she ever mention that to you?"

"No. We didn't talk about my sister. Everything I know about her disappearance came from listening to my mother on the phone . . . especially when they were fighting, because she yelled."

"Do you think your father could have kept your sister against your mother's will?"

"Mom was always very submissive toward him."

"Even after they split up?"

"It got better, but she was still very dependent. We relied on him entirely: none of us earned a cent."

"Do you think your sister could have gone looking for your father because she was pregnant?"

"It might have happened. My sister was always very dreamy; she could have been careless and . . ."

Letícia sat silently, fiddling with the wine glass, while Espinosa waited for her to finish the sentence.

"Is there anything else you've forgotten to tell me?"

"All I have are terrible nightmares. It's very hard to talk about these things . . . they're very close, familiar. . . . I get scared. Do you know what we're talking about? I'm talking about my father killing my boyfriend, my mother saying that my father was going to kill my sister, my mother threatening to go to the police, my mother getting killed . . . and even that Jonas is alive and . . ."

"We can talk again another time. Tomorrow. Later. Whenever you want."

The waiter came to the table, asked a question, got an unclear answer, and filled up the wine glasses again.

"Espinosa . . . do you think my father could have killed my mother?"

"Your father thinks Jonas killed her."

"Jonas is dead, Espinosa, get that through your head! Even if he was alive, why would he kill my mother, who never did anything to him?"

"Revenge."

"Revenge?"

"That's what your father thinks."

"That's crazy . . ."

Espinosa explained what her father thought: that Jonas, or Isidoro, had sought out the university hospital's treatment services as part of a plan to get close to him and then his family in order to destroy them, leaving Dr. Nesse to suffer the pain of having lost everyone close to him.

"That's a crazy idea!"

"Or it could be the idea of a crazy person."

Neither had touched the pizza. Espinosa's last remark had left Letícia silent. It was clear that the whole subject was painful and threatening for her. It was like opening the trunk hidden in the basement in a horror film.

"Do you want me to order a fresh pizza?"

"No. Thanks. I'm really not hungry. I'd better go home."

"Fine. I'll come with you."

"You didn't eat anything either."

"Don't worry, I'll eat later."

Espinosa asked for the check, and while they were waiting for the waiter he added: "You know you can call me at any time, day or night."

The guardian opened the door before Letícia had put her key into the lock. She was almost as young as Letícia.

———

The day began gray. The misty rain was barely heavy enough to reach the ground, and danced in the air to the tune of the cold wind blowing from the south. Espinosa walked from the Peixoto District to the station protected by the hood of his raincoat. He didn't like umbrellas; he didn't think they were much use in the tropics: too flimsy for a tropical storm and useless for that misty wind. Besides being, of course, just the kind of thing Espinosa left behind somewhere or another. At the station, Welber and Ramiro were drinking a liquid that seemed to be hot chocolate or tea with milk.

"It's starting to look like the Northern Hemisphere."

"What's looking like the Northern Hemisphere?"

"You two. What's that you're drinking?"

"Chocolate. Want some?"

"I'd rather have coffee."

"In the Northern Hemisphere they drink coffee too, Chief. Americans spend hours sipping that phony, weak stuff they call coffee. If it's going to be weak and phony, it's better to do like the English and have tea."

"So try a hot chocolate, boss. It's good for you: today the weather's more Chicago than Rio de Janeiro."

"Why Chicago?"

"Because they like hot chocolate there in the winter."

"Right."

Despite the rain and the cold, the chief was in a good mood. He didn't like umbrellas, but he did like rain and cold. Everyone agreed that he'd be better off in São Paulo, the only Northern Hemisphere city that had ended up in the Southern Hemisphere.

"This afternoon we're going to have our last conversation with Dr. Nesse."

"Why the last?"

"Because after that we won't be coming by to chat. I called his house, but nobody answered. I called his office and left a message on his machine."

"Any news?"

"Letícia called last night, scared, and wanted to talk."

"Did something happen to her?"

"I think so . . . at least, psychologically."

Espinosa told them about the talk in the restaurant, describing Letícia's state of mind and the terror that her own story caused her. He tried to reproduce her remarks as literally as possible.

"Until her mother's death, Letícia hadn't connected all the different strands of the story in which she herself was a central character. Her mother's murder was the link that allowed her to understand everything that had been happening over the last six or seven months. I don't think she'd put all the pieces together. Some parts of it are unbearable for her."

"From what I'm hearing," Welber interrupted, "we've got two completely different stories. Everything depends on whether Jonas is alive or dead."

"Right."

"So we've only got one, Chief, because the cadaver we saw in the cemetery in Pechincha is his," Ramiro said.

"His—whose?"

"Jonas's!"

"Ramiro, it's no use for you to be so convinced of that. You have to prove it."

"Prove what? That he's dead and buried?"

"No. Prove that he existed."

"Are you kidding, boss?"

"No."

"Chief—"

"Do you know his real name? His mother's name, his father's name? Any relatives? Anything that proves his identity? The image we have of the guy was constructed, fragment by fragment, from what Dr. Nesse told us. None of us has ever seen Jonas, Isidoro, or whatever his name is. The only thing you saw was a body in an advanced state of putrefaction, which you decided was Jonas because it had black hair. For us, Jonas is a ghost. A ghost almost entirely constructed by Dr. Nesse. Even the image Letícia provided was mostly a romantic take on the same image her dad had supplied. Jonas is nothing more than a character in different stories. He's as real as a flying saucer."

"But he existed. Tons of people saw him!"

"I don't know if the word 'existed' is quite right. Jonas was a succession of masks. It's not about searching for the true Jonas, or Isidoro, behind all the masks, but about figuring out which mask had some material reality and actually participated in the events we're investigating. And which one is a pure invention of the people implicated in the events."

"And the guy who's threatening Dr. Nesse?"

"The one from the square? Could be another mask, could be a lie."

"And the body from the cemetery?"

"I think it's probably the body of the person we're calling Jonas, but it's certainly not the same body that's threatening the doctor."

"Do you think that body died a natural death, like it says in the death certificate?"

"No."

"And Dona Teresa?"

"She surely didn't die a natural death."

"So . . ."

"So we'll have to have our last conversation with Dr. Nesse."

While the guardian was ordering lunch, Letícia went through the drawers in her mother's room, in search of the key. She didn't know if Roberta had a copy, but her mother had certainly kept a key to her ex-husband's apartment. She had insisted on it when they separated. "In case the girls need it," she'd said. It wasn't in the purse she usually carried, or inside any other purse. It wasn't a tough key to identify because it was on a key chain that featured a white plastic coin with the letter *A* printed on it in black. She found it inside a jewelry box, not at all hidden, on top of her mother's dresser. She stuck the key into her pants pocket and discreetly got ready, keeping her raincoat close by. Sooner or later the watchdog would have to go to the bathroom. The opportunity came after lunch when she went to brush her teeth and closed the door. Letícia turned on the TV, put on her coat, and left noiselessly. She hailed the first cab that passed. From a public phone, she called first her father's apartment and then his office. Nobody answered at the apartment, but at the office her father himself picked up. She didn't say anything.

She entered his building without being asked by anyone which apartment she was going to. Once inside, she had to act methodically. She'd never been there, so she didn't know where or how things were set up: all she knew was what she'd heard from her sister. She'd start in the bedroom, then proceed to the room he'd set aside for his daughters, and then check out the living room. She didn't have to rush, but she didn't want to risk being caught in the act.

When she opened the door, she thought she'd entered the wrong apartment. A rancid smell from the old take-out containers piled everywhere penetrated the whole space. She wanted to open the windows, but was afraid to draw the attention of the doorman or some curious neighbor. Since all the windows were covered by heavy curtains, she didn't think there'd be a problem if she turned on the lights.

She started in his room. She didn't know exactly what she was looking for, only that she needed clues—whether to prove his guilt or his innocence she wasn't sure. The first thing she found was the revolver. It was wrapped in a towel and hidden in the top of the wardrobe. Loaded. She left it where it was. In the drawer of the bedside table she found her sister's student ID card, and in a dresser drawer her address book. She didn't understand what they were doing there; or, rather, she understood but didn't want to accept it. It was irrefutable proof that her sister hadn't disappeared on the way to school or run off with her boyfriend, and that she hadn't been kidnapped. She searched the remaining drawers for a bag in which to stow her sister's belongings. It was incredible that her father could live in such a disgusting place. In the bathroom, among the dozens of free medicine samples her father had piled up inside the bathtub, she found the bag she needed. It wasn't empty, and before she dumped its contents into the bathtub, she checked to see if there was anything there that could break. What she found was a little bottle with a hypodermic needle and another bottle labeled POTASSIUM CHLORIDE. She took the bag to her father's room and deposited the objects on the bed. She felt like she was looking at a loaded weapon. She immediately recalled Espinosa's description of an injection of potassium chloride. She imagined her mother dashing out of their apartment after getting the phone call and pictured her walking toward the bench to meet her murderer. Whoever he was, she wouldn't have let him shoot her up with some unknown substance. She'd been doped, maybe with a powerful sleeping pill hidden in a warming drink, and readily been incorporated into the scene of a couple of lovers hugging on a bench while the potassium chloride was injected into her vein without anyone noticing. Letícia didn't want to continue her search. She grabbed her sister's backpack, which she'd spotted in the other room, returned to her father's room, and got the revolver out of the wardrobe. In the living room, she pushed everything from the table onto the floor. Then she arranged the syringe, the flask of potassium chloride, and her sister's ID and notebook upon the table. Before she left the apartment, she took his list of phone numbers and left the light on in the living room.

—

The misty rain continued all afternoon. After lunch, Espinosa called Dr. Nesse again. The machine picked up. The doctor might be with a client. If he was in the office, he would have heard the message Espinosa had left that morning, unless he was one of those people who forget to listen to their answering machine. Espinosa waited another half hour and called again. It was almost four in the afternoon, enough time for him to have seen his first patients of the afternoon and found a moment of opportunity to call the station. The phone rang four times, and Espinosa was about to give up when he heard the doctor's voice. His greeting sounded more like a supplication than a salutation.

"Dr. Nesse?"

"Yes."

"It's Chief Espinosa."

"Chief! He called again. . . . He wants to meet me . . ."

"Where and when?"

"Now . . ."

"Where?"

"I don't know."

"He didn't say?"

The call was cut off. Espinosa called back, but the line was busy. Maybe the doctor was on the phone with the station. After a few minutes passed without a call from Dr. Nesse, Espinosa tried the office again. Still busy. He decided to wait a few more minutes before calling back.

An incident involving a burglary that had turned violent forced him to leave the station. When he returned, he found a message on top of his desk, received half an hour earlier: "Chief Espinosa. Go immediately to Dr. Nesse's apartment. The key is under the doormat."

"Who left this message?"

"They didn't say."

"Man or woman?"

"I couldn't tell. The person was upset; it could have been a woman or a man crying. They just said it was urgent. They didn't give the address. They said you knew and then hung up."

"Welber, go see if there's a car available."

On the short trip from Copacabana to Ipanema, Espinosa imagined possible scenes that could await him in Dr. Nesse's apartment. In one of them, the doctor's dead body was stretched out on one of the chairs in the bedroom, with a needle in a vein; another was identical to the first, except with Jonas in place of the doctor; a third variation replaced the needle with a revolver, with a shot in the chest or the head; finally, there were versions with barbiturates, kitchen gas, and so on.

What the two cops found on the living room table dissolved all of Espinosa's fantasies and set off an alarm that made him whip around and run toward the elevator, pulling Welber by the arm.

"Quick! To his office!"

In the lobby of his building, they learned that the doctor had come in just a little before two, but none of the doormen knew if he was still there.

"I just know that nobody else was here."

"No client?"

"No, sir. That's why I don't know if he left or went to his office. But when he leaves in his car he goes straight to the garage, without coming through the lobby."

Espinosa and Welber went up and rang the bell. Nobody answered, and there was no note on the door announcing that Dr. Nesse was out. They kept ringing the bell. After a while, they went back to the lobby and asked the doorman to speak to the garage attendant.

"He says that Dr. Nesse's card is still there."

"What do you mean?"

"All the cars have a plastic card with the number of their space. When the car comes in, the card is placed on a board by the entrance and removed when he leaves. His is still there."

"Let's go talk to the attendant."

They left the lobby and made their way to the door of the garage via the sidewalk.

"Sometimes the doctor spends a few days without taking his car out. He really likes that big car, and only uses it when he needs to."

"And could he have left without taking the card?"

"No, sir, I'm the one who does that, not the driver. I don't open the door until I've taken it off."

"Where's his space?"

"Down the ramp, the third one after the elevator. There's no way to miss it."

The ramp was long; they ought to have taken the elevator. If any car came up the ramp, they'd have to mash themselves against the wall to let it pass. As they descended, the contrast grew between the light on the street and the badly lit garage, but their eyes quickly adapted. They arrived without incident at the end of the ramp and found the elevator door. The garage was packed at that hour, and even though their eyes were starting to get used to the dim light, it was still hard to distinguish between different cars.

Third space after the elevator. The car was parked in front of the wall. The well-polished metal reflected the light from the only bulb in that part of the garage. There was no doubt that it was the right car: its shiny chrome stood out from the less luxurious surrounding models. Before they had the chance to double-check the number of the space, Espinosa and Welber heard the sound of music. They looked behind them, trying to find where it was coming from, then immediately turned back to the car. There was a person sitting in the driver's seat, and the muffled music came from inside the car. Since they were approaching from behind, they couldn't see the person's face, only the shoulders and part of the head. A single, minuscule green light shone on the dashboard. When they approached, they saw that Dr. Nesse had his head on the headrest. The driver's window was open, and they could clearly make out the voice of a singer. Not wanting to startle the doctor, Espinosa called his name softly. No answer. Except for the unseen CD spinning inside the player, nothing was moving inside the car. Welber looked at Espinosa and opened the door. The inside light that came on revealed the red stain on the doctor's shirt.

Maria Callas was in the middle of her recital, and Dr. Nesse's body was still warm.

"He was taken by surprise. He still hadn't put his seat belt on. He must have turned on the ignition and then the stereo. The murderer must have turned off the engine."

"You said he was taken by surprise?"

"He didn't kill himself; he was murdered. There's no weapon here, and the shirt isn't even singed. The shot must have come from outside the car, with a small firearm, probably a .32. He must have rolled down the window to speak with the person before being shot without time to resist."

"Do you think that the fact that the window was down means he knew the person?"

"No. He could have rolled it down under duress."

"Professional?"

"I wouldn't bet on it. A pro would shoot for the head, with a more powerful weapon."

After calling the forensics team and canvassing the garage in search of someone who might have seen or heard something, Welber and Espinosa went back upstairs to talk with the garage attendant. He reported that several cars had come and gone in the last forty minutes—Espinosa had calculated how long the Maria Callas CD had been going—but that all of the incoming cars, or almost all of them, had gone to another floor, one above them.

"Did all the cars belong to people from the building?"

"Absolutely, sir. When someone from outside uses a place, the owner has to let us know in advance."

The elevator operators didn't recall any unfamiliar client, and hadn't seen anyone unusual on the garage floors. The doormen were even less helpful.

"Hundreds of people come through here every hour; any one of them could have gone down the stairs. They wouldn't need the elevator."

"Summing up," Espinosa said to Welber, "anyone could have gone down to the garage, waited next to his car—there isn't much light—and when Dr. Nesse got into the car and turned on the ignition and the stereo, could have approached and made him roll down the window. Once the job was done, they went back upstairs, walked through the lobby and onto the street."

"What worries me is that we've been following this guy for so long, thinking he's guilty, and in the end he wound up another victim. Just as, moreover, he'd always said."

"True. I just don't believe in the part about 'in the end.' "

"Well ... in a manner of speaking ... almost in the end."

"If you could tell me who killed Dr. Nesse, why, what happened to Jonas, who killed Dona Teresa, where Roberta went, then we could talk about the end."

"Do you think we're still at the beginning?"

"Not at the beginning, but we're still far from the end. If we ever get there."

They were in the lobby; it was past five o'clock, the traffic was building, and the forensics car would take a while to get in from Ipanema. Espinosa told Welber to let the attendant know that the forensics team would need access to the garage. As soon as he was alone, he called Letícia. The guardian answered.

"Chief, I'm so glad you called, Letícia ran out when I was in the bathroom. She's still not back. I can't reach Dr. Nesse."

"Wait for her to return. Take down my cell-phone number and call me when she does."

Espinosa asked the doorman for a copy of the key to Dr. Nesse's office, and the three of them went up.

The office was orderly. Espinosa took the doctor's scheduling book with all the clients' appointments and searched for a personal agenda or a phone book. He didn't find either, but in the drawer there were a few business cards. The two atop the pile were from a mechanic in Botafogo and a clinic in Méier. There were no messages on the machine. Espinosa asked Welber and the doorman to wait while he made a call. It didn't take more than two minutes.

"Welber, you wait here until forensics arrives. Get tape and isolate the scene of the crime. Make sure nobody touches anything until they get here. If Letícia shows up, which I don't think is going to happen, call me immediately."

"Where should I call?"

"My cell phone. Wait for me, even if it takes a while."

"Where are you going?"

"To Méier."

The house in the middle of the lot had originally had only two stories. When it was converted into a clinic, annexes had been added on the side and to the back, as had another parking area and a bright sign on the facade. It looked like a little hospital. Espinosa was greeted by the owner, whom he'd spoken to half an hour earlier.

"Sorry to keep you so long, Doctor."

"No problem, Officer: today's the day I always stay late. You said you were speaking from Dr. Nesse's office and that there'd been an accident."

"Not exactly an accident, Dr. . . ."

"Cerqueira."

"Dr. Cerqueira. Are you a friend of Dr. Nesse's?"

"We were at medical school together and did our residencies together."

"Why did he come looking for you, Doctor?"

"Because of his daughter. . . . That was such a tragedy. . . . I don't know how he managed to go on . . ."

"What happened?"

"She checked in with septicemia, general infection. . . . She was in a really bad state. She couldn't recover and died three days later."

"Why did he take her here instead of to some hospital closer by her home?"

"I think he didn't want to expose her."

"Expose her?"

"She'd had an abortion, Chief."

"Who performed it? Dr. Nesse himself?"

"No. Certainly not. She must have found some back-alley abortionist. All I knew was that she'd had a hemorrhage followed by an infection. There wasn't much we could do. She didn't react to the antibiotics. She was only a girl."

"Did she say something?"

"She said something about the child being cursed. When I asked her what she meant, she didn't say anything else."

"How did you . . ."

"We diagnosed her with septicemia. There was no need to make the parents suffer more with a criminal process. Artur Nesse took care of the burial the next day. I don't even know how they're dealing with it."

"They're not, Doctor."

"What . . . ?"

"They're both dead."

"Dead?"

"Murdered."

"Holy shit!"

"That's why I needed to talk to you personally, not over the phone."

"Who killed them?"

"She was killed on a park bench near her house; he was killed in his car, inside the garage of the building where he worked. Nobody saw anything in either case. Did he say anything about being stalked?"

"Stalked?"

"He told me he was being stalked by a client, a psychopath."

"He didn't say anything to me. He was so devastated

by the situation that we hardly spoke. He scarcely said a word. Holy shit! A patient!"

"We don't know if he did it."

"You can't speak to him?"

"He disappeared."

"So . . ."

"More than five months ago. We don't even know if he's still alive."

When he got back to Ipanema, Espinosa entered the garage with the feeling that he was stumbling onto a film set, there were so many people and lights. Ramiro and Welber were talking near the car, while Freire was dismounting one of the portable reflectors he'd brought. The inspector and the detective came to greet Espinosa as soon as they saw him emerge from the elevator.

"Any news of Letícia?"

"Nothing, Chief."

"Welber, call the guardian and see if she can spend the night in the apartment and wait for Letícia to come back."

Espinosa was glad to hear that the forensic testing was being taken care of by Freire, one of the best technicians from the Criminological Institute and an old acquaintance. The technician was already gathering up his things when Espinosa walked over to him.

"Hey, Freire."

"Hey, Espinosa."

"Anything useful?"

"A shot, close by, fired from above, no cartridge found, probable weapon .32 revolver, only one kind of finger-print on the door and the handle. Details after we retrieve the bullet."

It wasn't a short report: that was how Freire talked. He tried to conserve his words as much as possible. He had long since eliminated the use of adjectives. He was still working on eliminating articles, prepositions, and adverbs. The chief thought he wasn't far away from his goal.

Welber came over to say that the guardian had agreed to wait for Letícia.

"Have you eaten?"

"No, sir."

"Then let's go find a place that serves a decent sand-wich."

"By decent sandwich do you mean one of those with two layers of cheese plus layers of hamburger, cream sauce, mustard, ketchup, and a little piece of lettuce, just to pretend you're eating something besides plastic?"

"Give it up, Welber, you won't manage to ruin it for me."

"Far be it, boss, I'm just trying to save your life."

Across the square was a luncheonette that offered exactly the kind of sandwich Welber had described. Welber chose the light version.

"Did you get anything in Méier?"

"Roberta's dead. She died of a general infection as the

consequence of an abortion. Your first guess was right, Ramiro. But the ending, unfortunately, was different."

"Why Méier?"

Espinosa told what he'd learned from the director of the clinic.

"And the body?"

"She was buried the next day, in the cemetery in Caju. According to the doctor, the only people present were him, Dr. Nesse, and Dona Teresa."

"And she must have told her ex-husband that she'd go to the police."

"And he killed her. Probably the night of the same day they buried their daughter. He couldn't take the chance."

It was almost ten that evening when Dr. Nesse's body was taken to the Forensic Institute. Ramiro and Welber stayed close to the garage exit, stopping every car and asking if they'd seen or heard anything suspicious around five that afternoon, near the elevator door on the first floor. Nobody had. When all the cars had left the building, the two cops were worn out from asking the same questions and getting the same answers.

"So?" asked Espinosa.

"Nobody saw anything. I don't even think they saw cars in the parking garage."

"You'd better go on home, then."

"Don't worry, Chief, we can get the subway until eleven."

The three of them stood on the sidewalk in front of the building, with their backs to the station's car.

"Let's go to the bar on the corner and have some coffee."

"Good idea—otherwise we'll fall asleep on the train."

"No news from Letícia?" Ramiro asked.

"No, but I think she'll go back home tonight."

"Why do you think that?"

"Because she'll get tired of walking around, because she doesn't have anywhere to sleep, and because she needs to be in her room to be able to think things over."

"So she's already heard about her father's death?"

"Surely."

"And how did she find out?"

"She was there."

"She was there? She saw her father being killed? How do you know that?"

"I still need to check out one more thing . . . as soon as we find Letícia."

~

Ramiro and Welber returned to Copacabana to leave the car at the station and take the subway to Tijuca. Espinosa had a final cup of coffee, went back to the office building, and left his card with his cell-phone number written on it with the doorman, "in case anyone shows up saying they're a friend or relative of Dr. Nesse's." The probability was remote, but he didn't want to ignore it.

He took the Rua Francisco Sá toward the beach, continuing down the Avenida Atlântica. The idea was to keep walking to the Peixoto District, in an attempt to relax or simply wear himself out before going to sleep—which didn't exclude the possibility of visiting Letícia's building, a few blocks away from his own. It would be a total of about two kilometers, halfway down the beach. The temperature was pleasant and he'd have plenty of time to think about the events of that afternoon. He was walking slowly, but a half hour later he was already ringing the doorbell of Letícia's apartment. The guardian answered, frightened and feeling responsible for Letícia's disappearance.

"Don't blame yourself. At some point you would have had to leave her alone."

"I should have locked the door and kept the key."

"She could have gotten desperate and jumped out of the window."

"Do you think she could—"

"Probably not, since she left through the door."

Espinosa told the girl about Dr. Nesse's death, without adding that he'd been murdered and without mentioning Roberta's death. He also told her that Letícia had somehow found out about what happened and that she'd been missing ever since.

"I think she's out there, wandering around, or maybe

she went to see some friend, maybe someone from school, to talk to. Maybe she'll come back tonight or tomorrow morning. If that happens, no matter how late it is, call me."

There was no call that night, and by ten o'clock the next morning Letícia still hadn't returned home. Ramiro and Welber called the hospitals and talked to the police in other precincts. Nothing involving a young girl matching Letícia's description had been noted in the last twenty-four hours. She had disappeared.

At ten-thirty, Espinosa called Welber and had him check to see if there were any cars available. The detective was back in less than a minute.

"The car's ready, Chief."

"You drive."

"Where to?"

"The psychiatric hospital."

Since the boss didn't add anything else, Welber didn't pose any questions. They drove in silence to the university. It was the busiest time of day on campus, and they had trouble parking. They found a place far from the hospital entrance and headed toward the hospital under the pleasant winter sun.

"What are you looking for, Chief?"

"The tree . . . and the stone bench where Dr. Nesse said Jonas sat."

"Do you think Letícia's here?"

"It's very possible."

"Why?"

"Because the person who killed Dr. Nesse didn't kill him to rob him. His wallet was in his coat pocket. His watch was expensive, and it was on his wrist. It wasn't a hired gun, either. A pro would go for the head and use a more powerful weapon. If you're standing up, a little bit squeezed between two cars and only a couple of feet away from where the victim is seated behind the steering wheel, the easiest place to hit is the head. If, instead of that, you go for the chest, that's because you don't want to destroy the victim's face."

"Why wouldn't you want to hit the face?"

"Because it was a familiar face."

They proceeded through the iron gates into the hospital, and Welber pointed at the top of the great mango tree, visible in the distance. As they came closer, they could see more of the tree, and beneath it, the stone bench.

Letícia was there, her feet resting on the big root, grasping in her lap something that looked like a backpack. Espinosa sat beside her, while Welber walked to the lobby of the hospital. She didn't show surprise or any other emotion.

"What are you doing here, Letícia?"

"Waiting."

"Waiting for whom?"

"Jonas."

"And do you think he'll turn up here?"

"This is his place."

"But it's not yours."

"Why not?"

"You've got your house."

"Not anymore. My mother's dead and I'm not going to live with my father even if I'm forced to. My place is here. With Jonas."

"But Jonas isn't here anymore."

"This is where he liked to be. He'll come back."

"You don't want to go back home, take a shower, change clothes . . ."

"When Jonas gets here."

Welber came back, accompanied by a doctor. Espinosa got up to greet them, moving out of Letícia's earshot.

"Sir, this is Dr. Fraga. He's familiar with the whole Jonas story and knows about the episode Letícia was involved in. He also knows that she's Dr. Nesse's daughter. She's been here since yesterday afternoon. They managed to find a place for her to sleep in one of the waiting rooms. She says she's waiting for Jonas."

"What sort of condition is she in?"

"She's in a psychotic state. It might be temporary or it might not be—hard to say."

"She lost her father, her mother, and her sister in less than a week."

"That's why I'm saying it might be temporary. It might be her way of denying those deaths, and that's why she says she's waiting for the kid . . . who died as well. But we can't forget that she already had another psychotic crisis, months ago, that led her to be interned here at this hospital."

"Couldn't it have been her reaction to a shocking event?"

"Sir, people experience shocking events every day, some extremely violent, but they don't all end up psychotic."

"Do you think she's ill?"

"It's still too early to say. Let's wait a few days. We'll take good care of her, don't worry."

"I know she has some relatives, but I don't know who they are or where they live. Until we track some of them down, the hospital can get in touch with me for anything you need."

Espinosa excused himself to sit alone with Letícia for a few minutes under the mango tree. The doctor said his farewells and went back to the main building with Welber. Espinosa sat back down beside her.

"Letícia, the doctors and nurses are going to take care of you while you wait for Jonas to get here. You can call me whenever you want. And I'll come see you here whenever I can. Is that okay?"

"Yes."

"Can I see your backpack to see if everything is okay?"

Letícia handed him the backpack, with her eyes cast down toward her tennis shoe, which she was rubbing on the tree root. At the bottom of the backpack, wrapped in a sweater, Espinosa found the revolver. He placed it in his handkerchief and put it into his coat pocket.

The trip back to the station was made in silence. Welber wanted to ask questions, but he knew Espinosa well enough to know that he wouldn't get more than mono-syllables in return. As soon as they were back at the station, Ramiro joined them and they sat down in the chief's small office, with the computer as a silent witness.

Espinosa reported what had happened during their meeting with Letícia, which Welber had not observed in its entirety, and spoke of the revolver he'd found in her backpack.

"We've got enough proof to open proceedings, even though nothing concrete would come of it. Of the five people directly involved, the only one who's alive and the author of one of the murders is impossible to prose-cute . . . and has already been handed down the worst sentence. But more than clarifying who's guilty, an inves-tigation could clear the names of the people who were mere victims."

"And what about Jonas?" Welber asked.

"I think that in terms of Jonas a whole lot is going to remain guesswork. I think he was the victim of Dr. Nesse's paranoia. Because of something—we'll never know what, it could have been something Jonas said or some physi-cal characteristic—the doctor imagined that Jonas was stalking him, and after Jonas met Letícia, he imagined that Jonas was attacking the whole Nesse family. The things Dr. Nesse said Jonas did could indeed have happened, or they could have been part of the doctor's delirium. What's not true is the motive the doctor ascribed to Jonas's behavior. The delirium culminated with Jonas's being transferred to the general hospital to do some tests and receiving the potassium chloride solution prepared by Dr. Nesse. Left without identification on a cot in a hallway in the hospital, he was determined to have suffered cardiac arrest and was buried as a pauper. It might not have happened exactly like that. There are some blanks we'll never be able to fill in. That's it."

"And what's going to happen to Letícia?" Welber asked.

"It's already happened."

ABOUT THE AUTHOR

A distinguished academic, LUIZ ALFREDO GARCIA-ROZA is a best-selling novelist who lives in Rio de Janeiro. The first book in the Espinosa series, *The Silence of the Rain,* was published in 2002 by Henry Holt to critical acclaim, followed by *December Heat* (2003), *Southwesterly Wind* (2004), and *A Window in Copacabana* (2005). All four books are available in paperback from Picador. Garcia-Roza is currently at work on a new detective series.